Dance Class

Crip • Art
Béka • Story
Benoît Bekaert • Color

PAPERCUTZ™
New York

Dance Class
Graphic Novels Available from PAPERCUTZ™

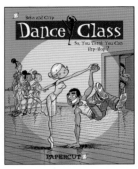
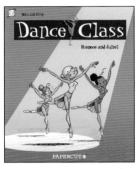

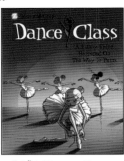
Dance Class

Studio Danse [Dance Class], by Béka & Crip
© 2008 BAMBOO ÉDITION.
www.bamboo.fr

DANCE CLASS #1
"So, You Think You Can Hip-Hop?"

Béka - writer
Crip - Artist
Benoît Bekaert - Colorist
Joe Johnson - Translation
Sylvia Nantier - Dance Consultant
Tom Orzechowski - Lettering
Nelson Design Group, LLC - Production
Michael Petranek - Associate Editor
Jim Salicrup
Editor-in-Chief

ISBN: 978-1-59707-254-0

Printed in China
August 2012 by New Era Printing, LTD
Unit C, 8/F, Worldwide Centre
123 Tung Chau St
Kowloon, Hong Kong

Distributed by Macmillan.
Second Papercutz Printing

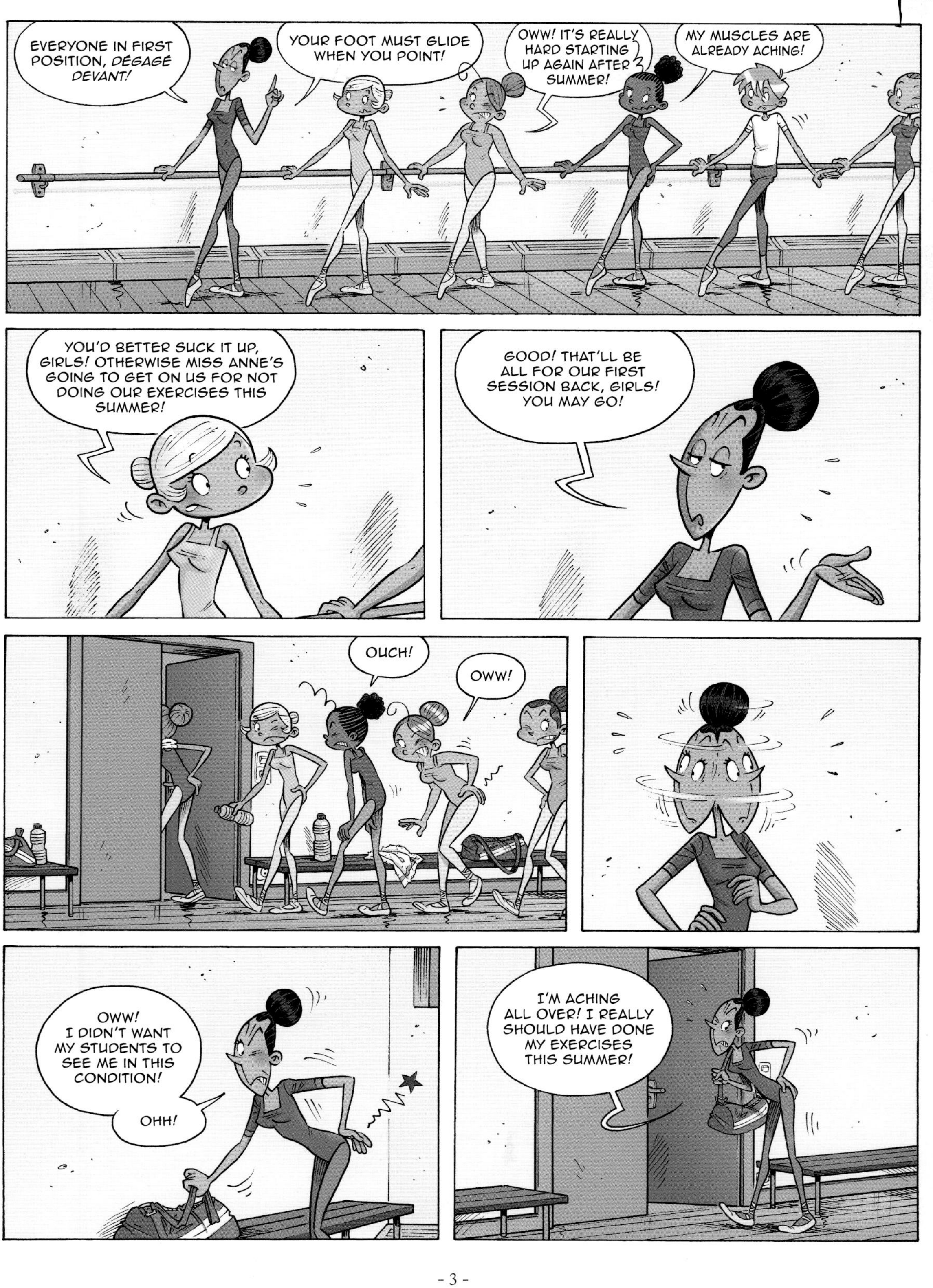
EVERYONE IN FIRST POSITION, *DÉGAGÉ DEVANT!*
YOUR FOOT MUST GLIDE WHEN YOU POINT!
OWW! IT'S REALLY HARD STARTING UP AGAIN AFTER SUMMER!
MY MUSCLES ARE ALREADY ACHING!
YOU'D BETTER SUCK IT UP, GIRLS! OTHERWISE MISS ANNE'S GOING TO GET ON US FOR NOT DOING OUR EXERCISES THIS SUMMER!
GOOD! THAT'LL BE ALL FOR OUR FIRST SESSION BACK, GIRLS! YOU MAY GO!
OUCH!
OWW!
OWW! I DIDN'T WANT MY STUDENTS TO SEE ME IN THIS CONDITION!
OHH!
I'M ACHING ALL OVER! I REALLY SHOULD HAVE DONE MY EXERCISES THIS SUMMER!

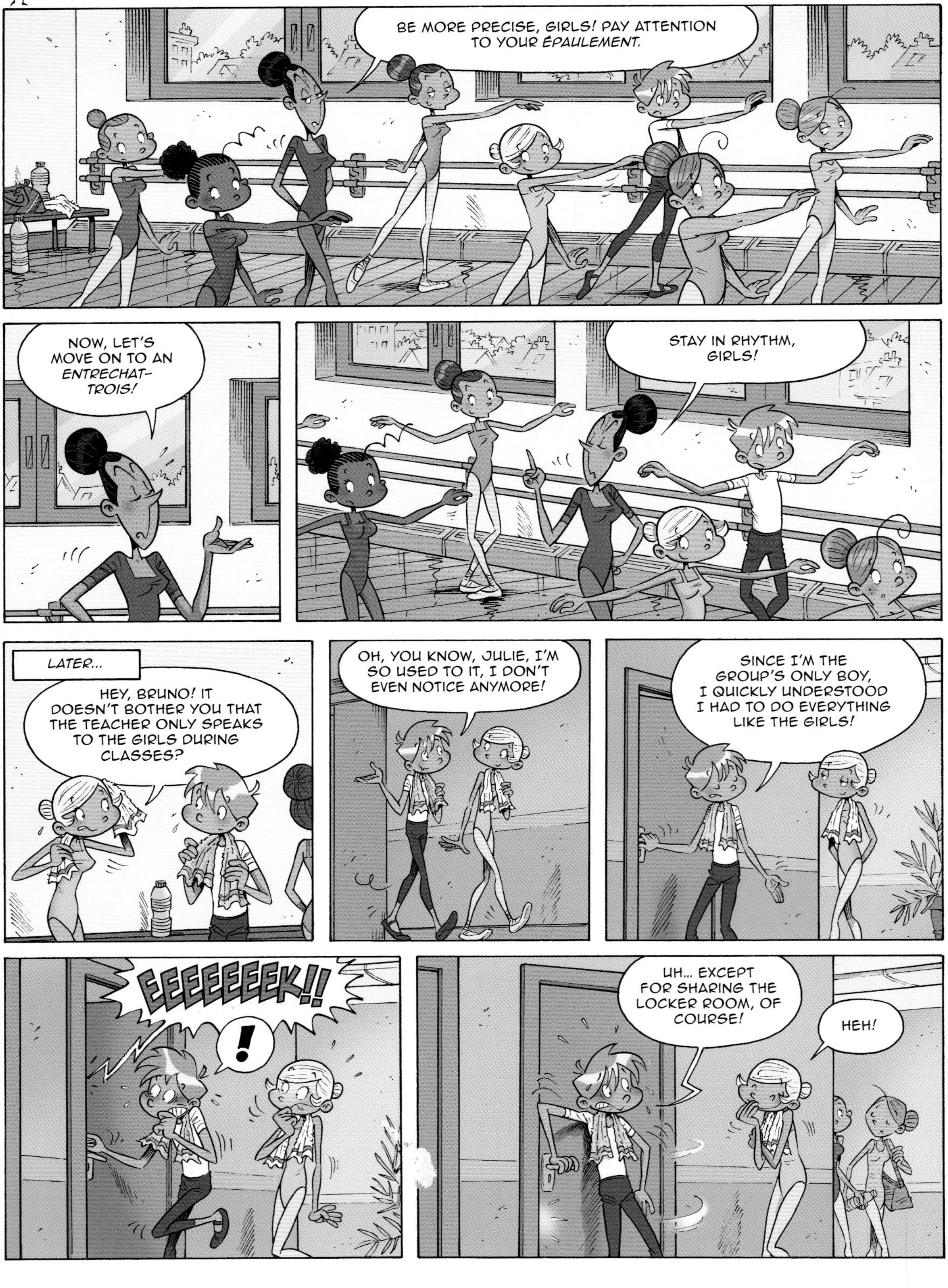
BE MORE PRECISE, GIRLS! PAY ATTENTION TO YOUR *ÉPAULEMENT*.
NOW, LET'S MOVE ON TO AN *ENTRECHAT-TROIS*!
STAY IN RHYTHM, GIRLS!
LATER...
HEY, BRUNO! IT DOESN'T BOTHER YOU THAT THE TEACHER ONLY SPEAKS TO THE GIRLS DURING CLASSES?
OH, YOU KNOW, JULIE, I'M SO USED TO IT, I DON'T EVEN NOTICE ANYMORE!
SINCE I'M THE GROUP'S ONLY BOY, I QUICKLY UNDERSTOOD I HAD TO DO EVERYTHING LIKE THE GIRLS!
EEEEEEEK!!
!
UH... EXCEPT FOR SHARING THE LOCKER ROOM, OF COURSE!
HEH!

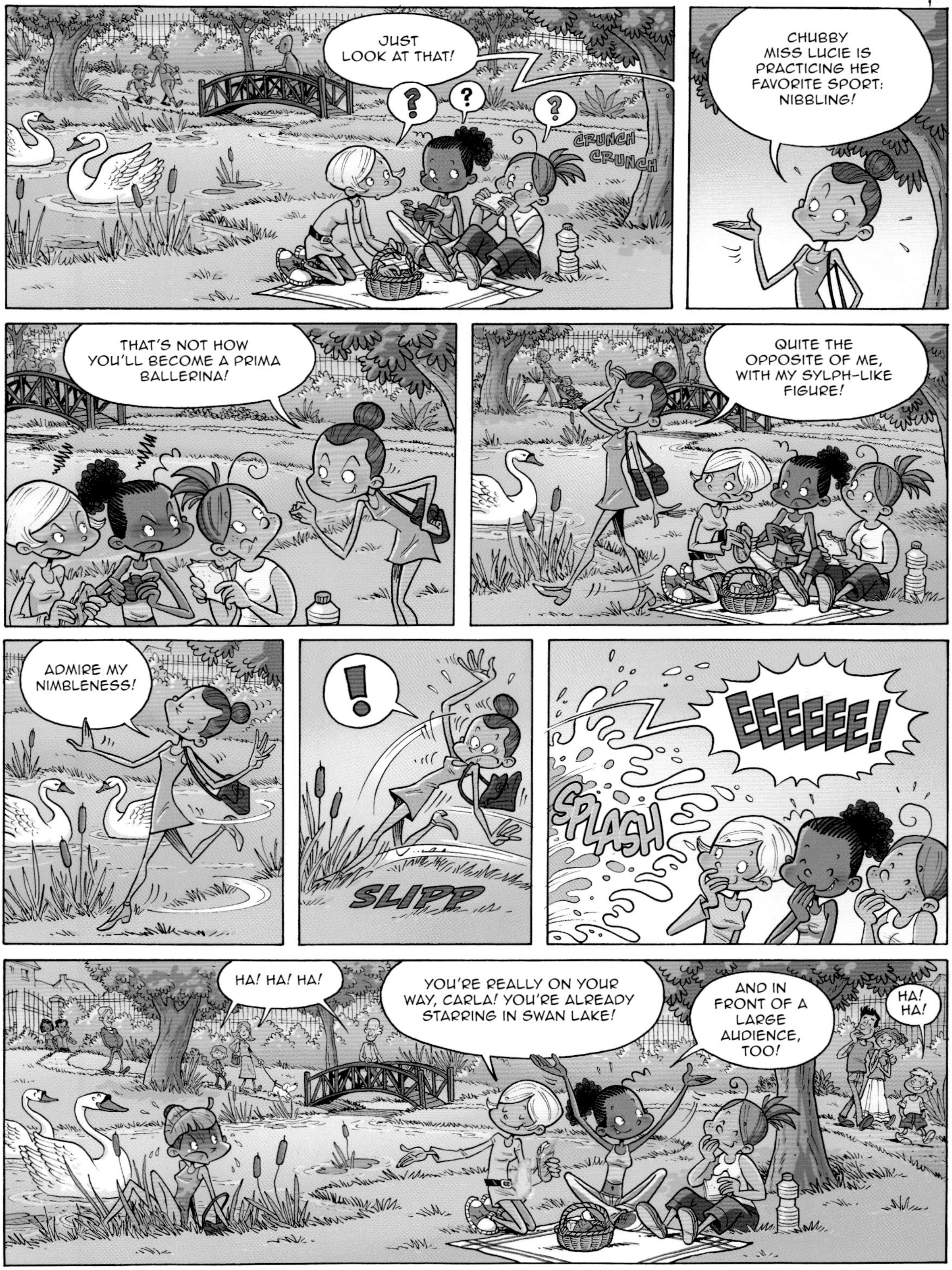
JUST LOOK AT THAT!
?
?
?
CRUNCH CRUNCH
CHUBBY MISS LUCIE IS PRACTICING HER FAVORITE SPORT: NIBBLING!
THAT'S NOT HOW YOU'LL BECOME A PRIMA BALLERINA!
QUITE THE OPPOSITE OF ME, WITH MY SYLPH-LIKE FIGURE!
ADMIRE MY NIMBLENESS!
!
SLIPP
EEEEEE!
SPLASH
HA! HA! HA!
YOU'RE REALLY ON YOUR WAY, CARLA! YOU'RE ALREADY STARRING IN SWAN LAKE!
AND IN FRONT OF A LARGE AUDIENCE, TOO!
HA! HA!

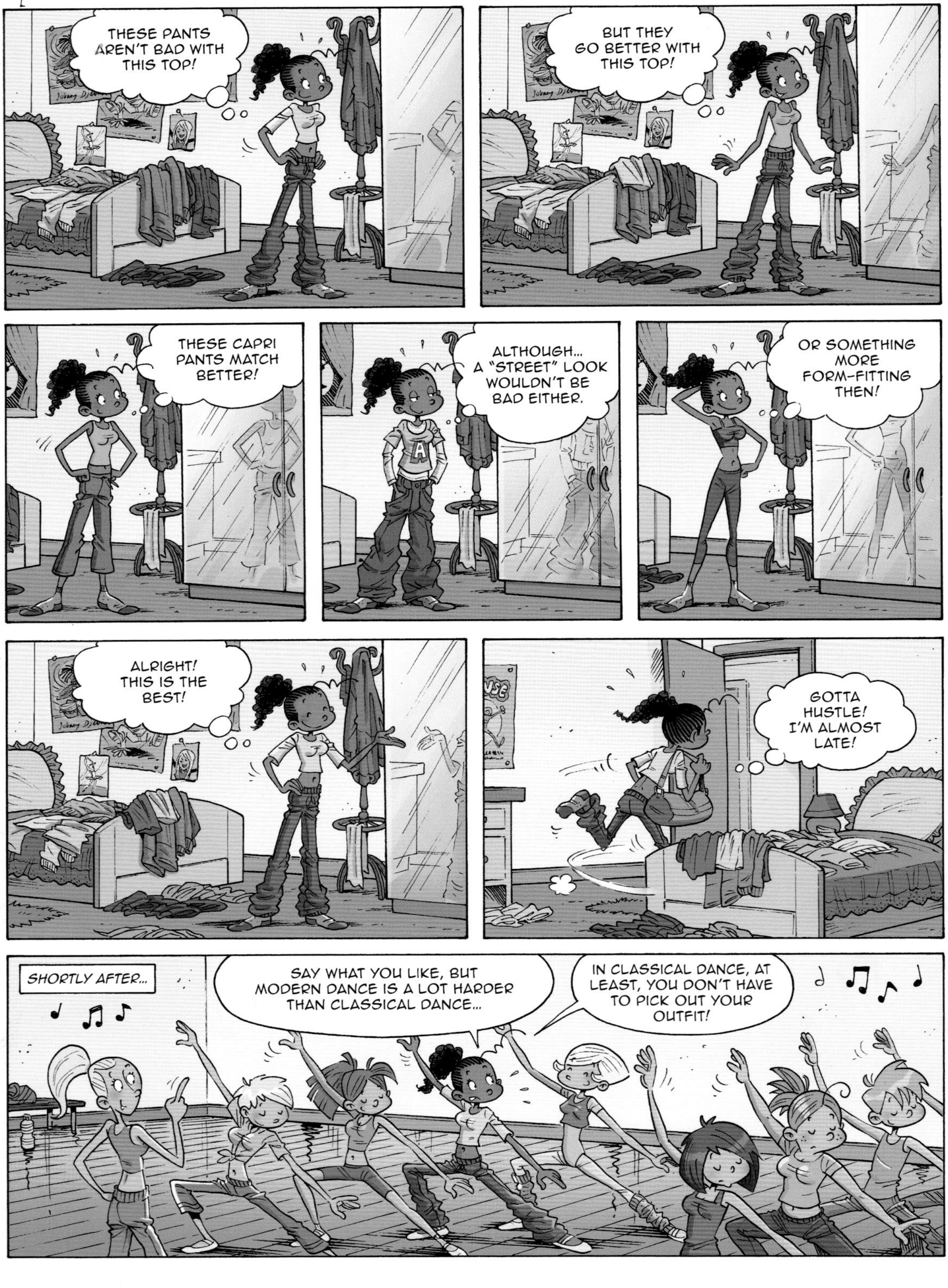
THESE PANTS AREN'T BAD WITH THIS TOP!
BUT THEY GO BETTER WITH THIS TOP!
THESE CAPRI PANTS MATCH BETTER!
ALTHOUGH... A "STREET" LOOK WOULDN'T BE BAD EITHER.
OR SOMETHING MORE FORM-FITTING THEN!
ALRIGHT! THIS IS THE BEST!
GOTTA HUSTLE! I'M ALMOST LATE!
SHORTLY AFTER...
SAY WHAT YOU LIKE, BUT MODERN DANCE IS A LOT HARDER THAN CLASSICAL DANCE...
IN CLASSICAL DANCE, AT LEAST, YOU DON'T HAVE TO PICK OUT YOUR OUTFIT!

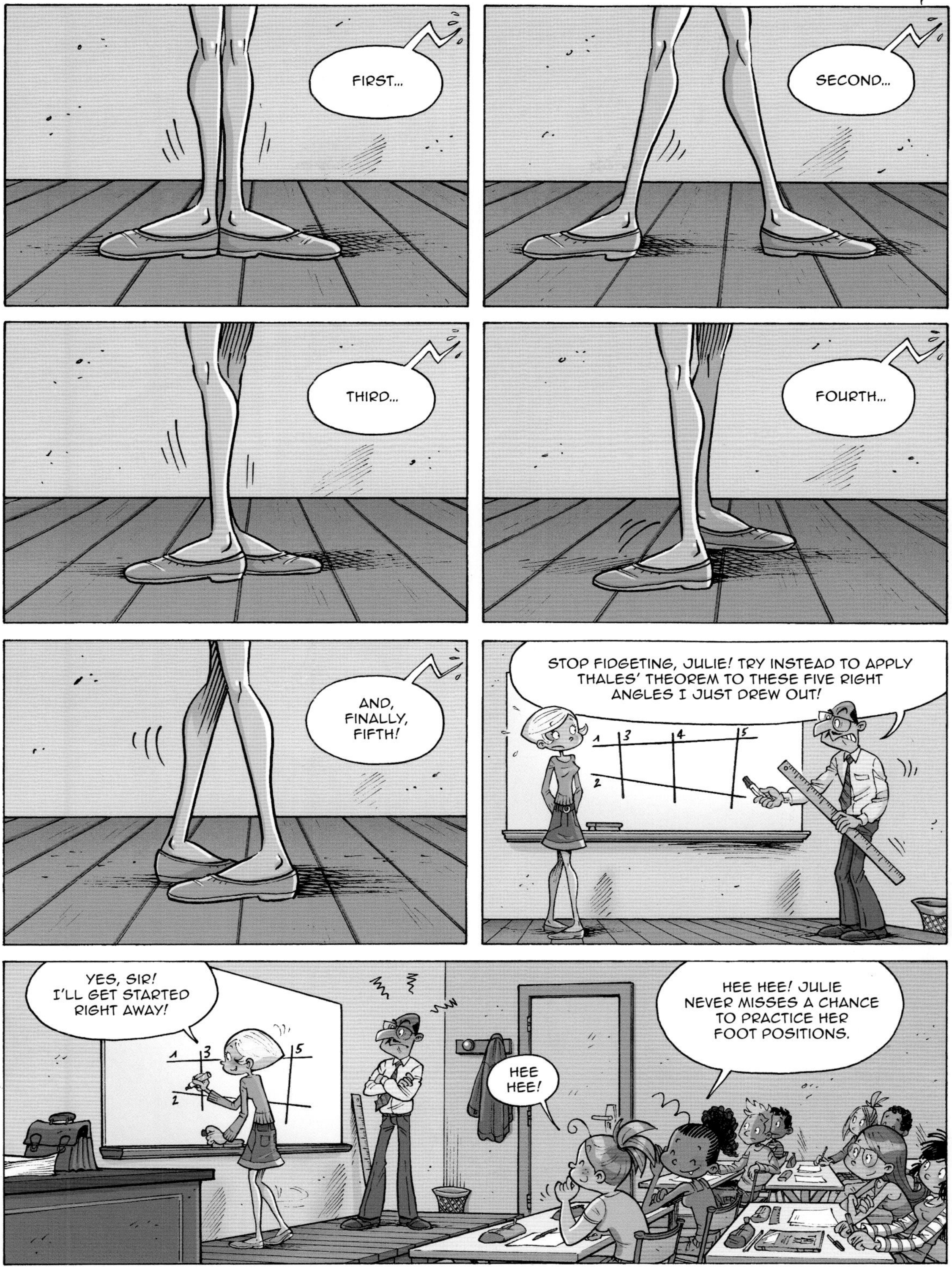
FIRST...
SECOND...
THIRD...
FOURTH...
AND, FINALLY, FIFTH!
STOP FIDGETING, JULIE! TRY INSTEAD TO APPLY THALES' THEOREM TO THESE FIVE RIGHT ANGLES I JUST DREW OUT!
YES, SIR! I'LL GET STARTED RIGHT AWAY!
HEE HEE!
HEE HEE! JULIE NEVER MISSES A CHANCE TO PRACTICE HER FOOT POSITIONS.

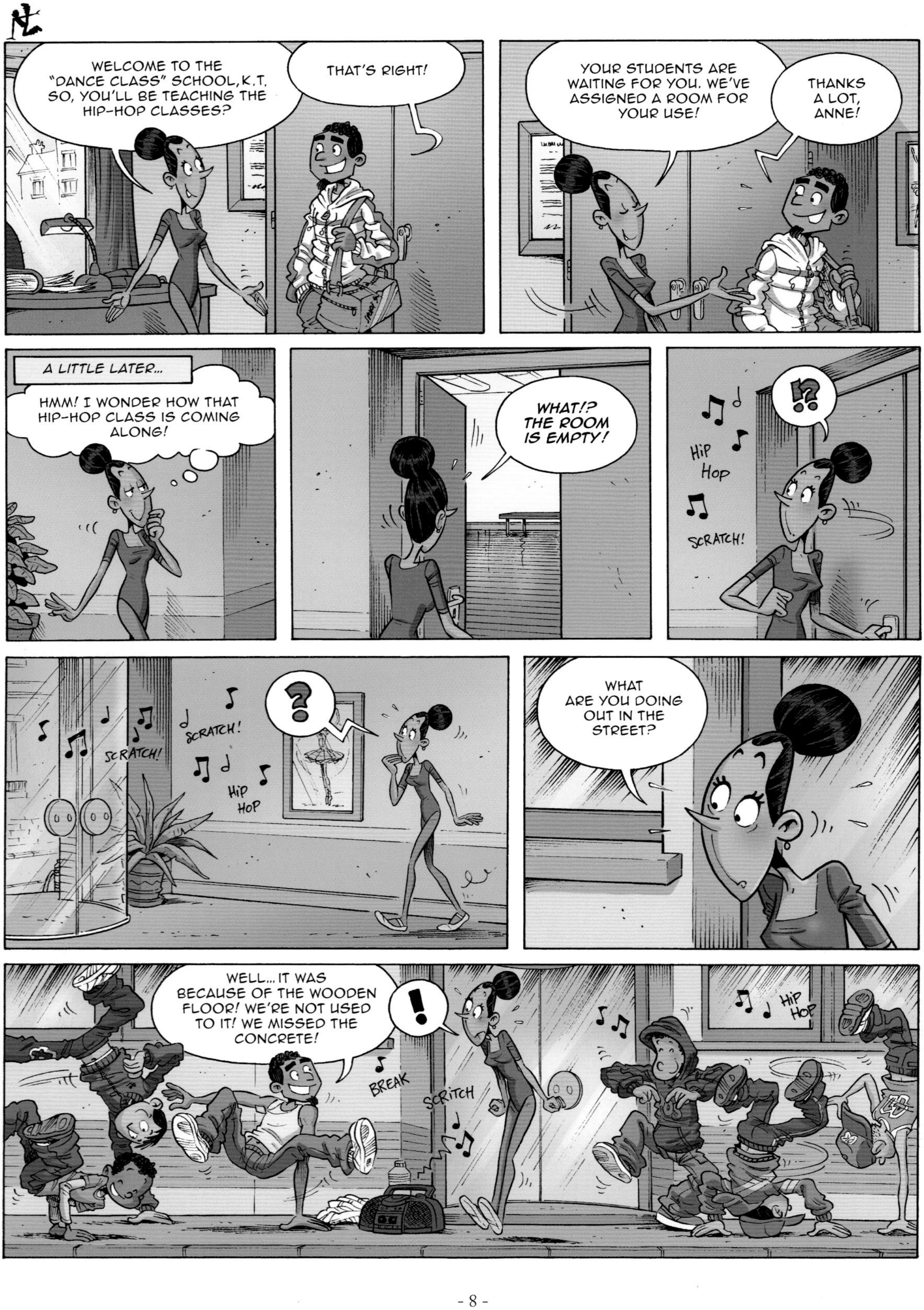
WELCOME TO THE "DANCE CLASS" SCHOOL, K.T. SO, YOU'LL BE TEACHING THE HIP-HOP CLASSES?
THAT'S RIGHT!
YOUR STUDENTS ARE WAITING FOR YOU. WE'VE ASSIGNED A ROOM FOR YOUR USE!
THANKS A LOT, ANNE!
A LITTLE LATER...
HMM! I WONDER HOW THAT HIP-HOP CLASS IS COMING ALONG!
WHAT!? THE ROOM IS EMPTY!
HIP HOP
SCRATCH!
SCRATCH!
SCRATCH!
HIP HOP
WHAT ARE YOU DOING OUT IN THE STREET?
WELL... IT WAS BECAUSE OF THE WOODEN FLOOR! WE'RE NOT USED TO IT! WE MISSED THE CONCRETE!
BREAK
SCRITCH
HIP HOP

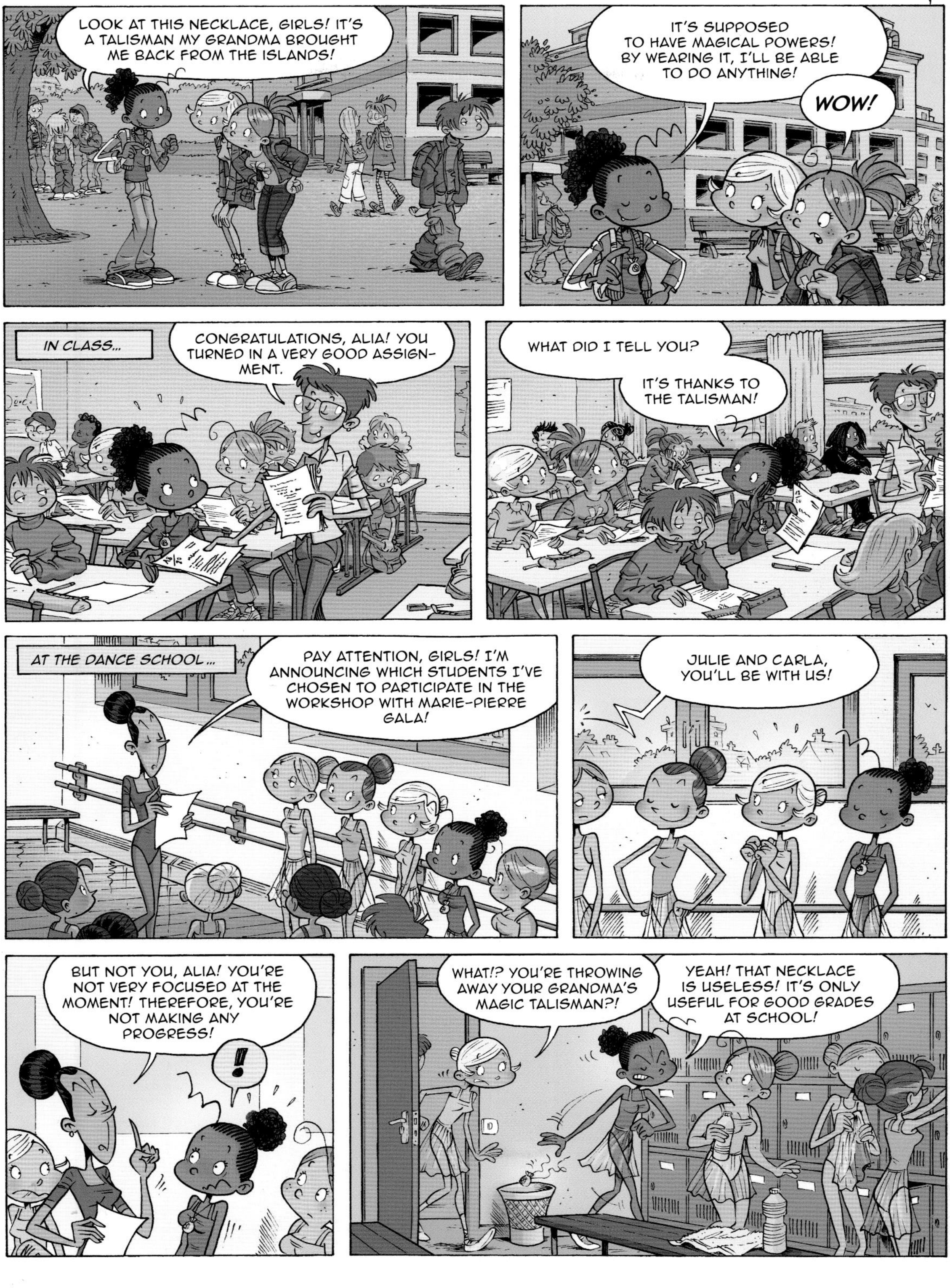
LOOK AT THIS NECKLACE, GIRLS! IT'S A TALISMAN MY GRANDMA BROUGHT ME BACK FROM THE ISLANDS!
IT'S SUPPOSED TO HAVE MAGICAL POWERS! BY WEARING IT, I'LL BE ABLE TO DO ANYTHING!
WOW!
IN CLASS...
CONGRATULATIONS, ALIA! YOU TURNED IN A VERY GOOD ASSIGNMENT.
WHAT DID I TELL YOU?
IT'S THANKS TO THE TALISMAN!
AT THE DANCE SCHOOL...
PAY ATTENTION, GIRLS! I'M ANNOUNCING WHICH STUDENTS I'VE CHOSEN TO PARTICIPATE IN THE WORKSHOP WITH MARIE-PIERRE GALA!
JULIE AND CARLA, YOU'LL BE WITH US!
BUT NOT YOU, ALIA! YOU'RE NOT VERY FOCUSED AT THE MOMENT! THEREFORE, YOU'RE NOT MAKING ANY PROGRESS!
!
WHAT!? YOU'RE THROWING AWAY YOUR GRANDMA'S MAGIC TALISMAN?!
YEAH! THAT NECKLACE IS USELESS! IT'S ONLY USEFUL FOR GOOD GRADES AT SCHOOL!

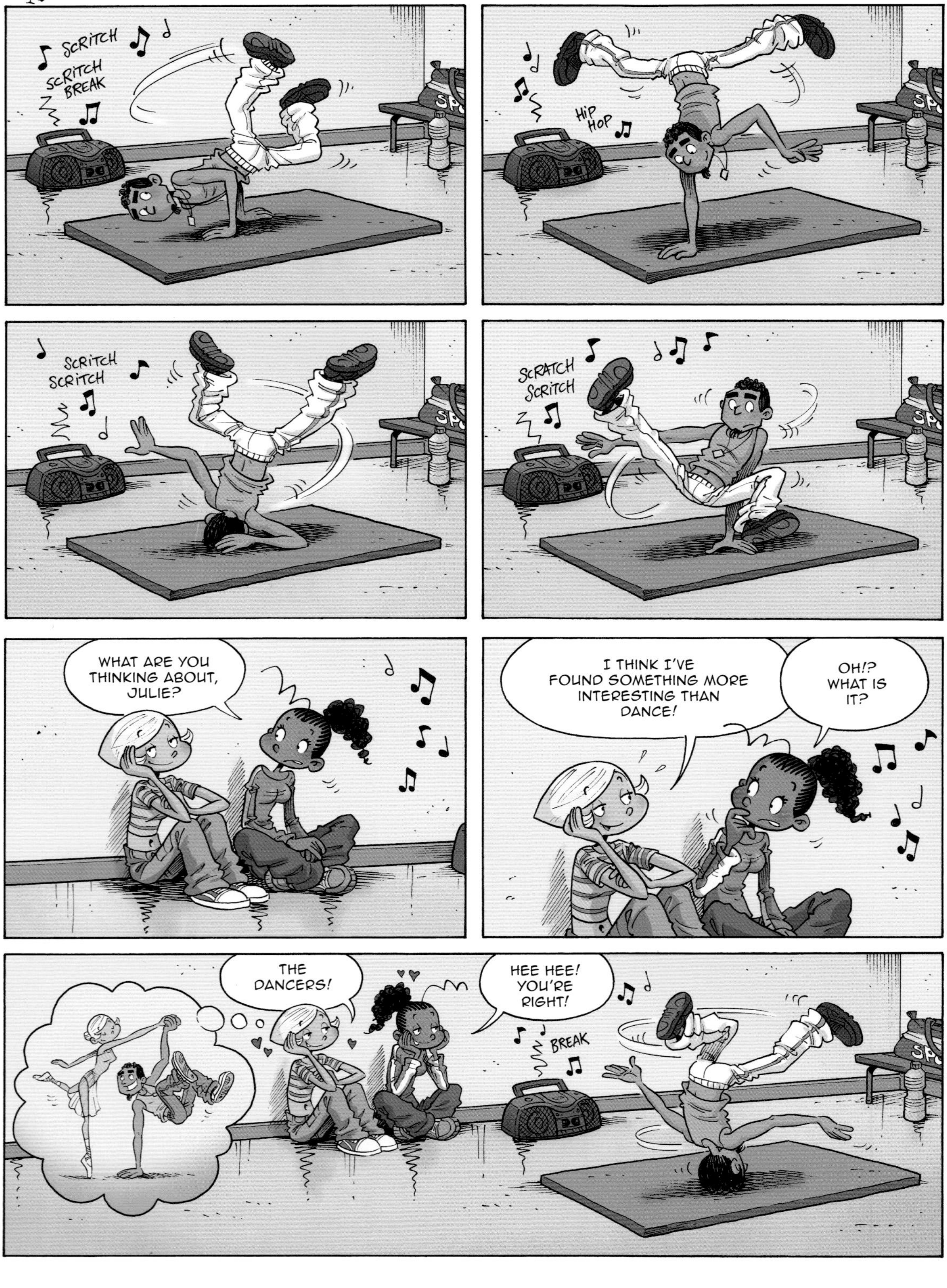
SCRITCH
SCRITCH BREAK
HIP HOP
SCRITCH SCRITCH
SCRATCH SCRITCH
WHAT ARE YOU THINKING ABOUT, JULIE?
I THINK I'VE FOUND SOMETHING MORE INTERESTING THAN DANCE!
OH!? WHAT IS IT?
THE DANCERS!
HEE HEE! YOU'RE RIGHT!
BREAK

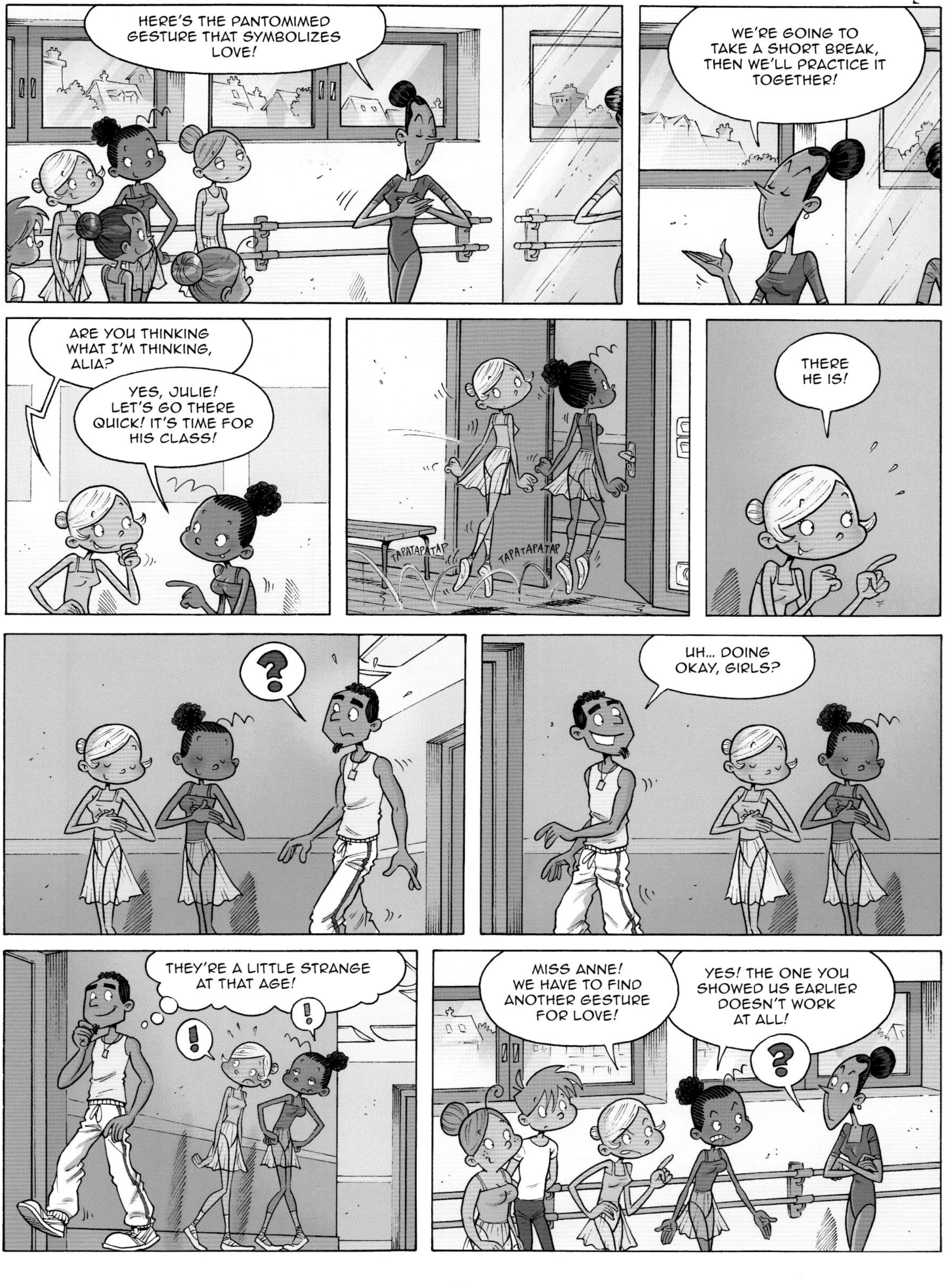
HERE'S THE PANTOMIMED GESTURE THAT SYMBOLIZES LOVE!
WE'RE GOING TO TAKE A SHORT BREAK, THEN WE'LL PRACTICE IT TOGETHER!
ARE YOU THINKING WHAT I'M THINKING, ALIA?
YES, JULIE! LET'S GO THERE QUICK! IT'S TIME FOR HIS CLASS!
TAPATAPATAP
TAPATAPATAP
THERE HE IS!
?
UH... DOING OKAY, GIRLS?
THEY'RE A LITTLE STRANGE AT THAT AGE!
!
!
MISS ANNE! WE HAVE TO FIND ANOTHER GESTURE FOR LOVE!
YES! THE ONE YOU SHOWED US EARLIER DOESN'T WORK AT ALL!
?

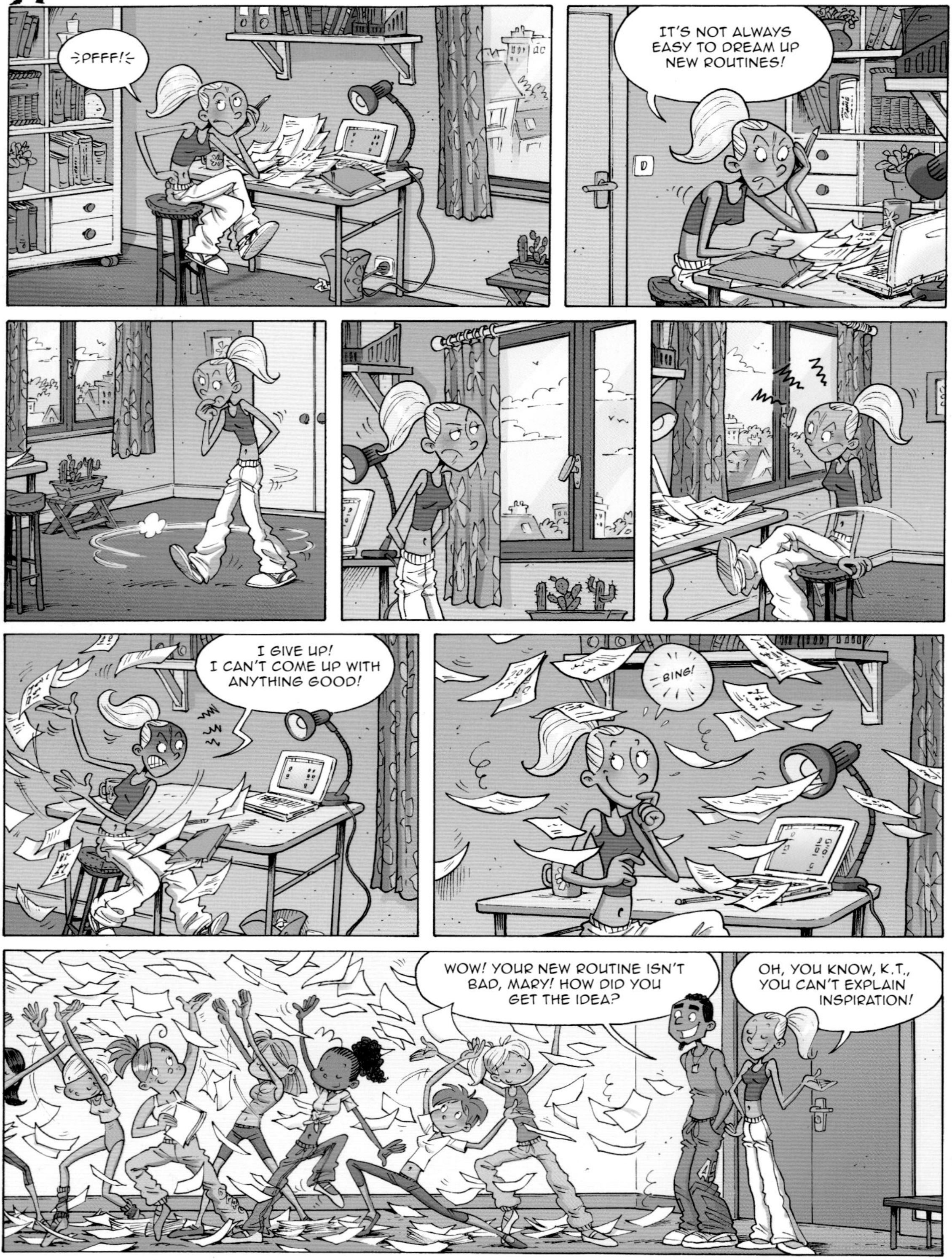
PFFF!
IT'S NOT ALWAYS EASY TO DREAM UP NEW ROUTINES!
I GIVE UP! I CAN'T COME UP WITH ANYTHING GOOD!
BING!
WOW! YOUR NEW ROUTINE ISN'T BAD, MARY! HOW DID YOU GET THE IDEA?
OH, YOU KNOW, K.T., YOU CAN'T EXPLAIN INSPIRATION!

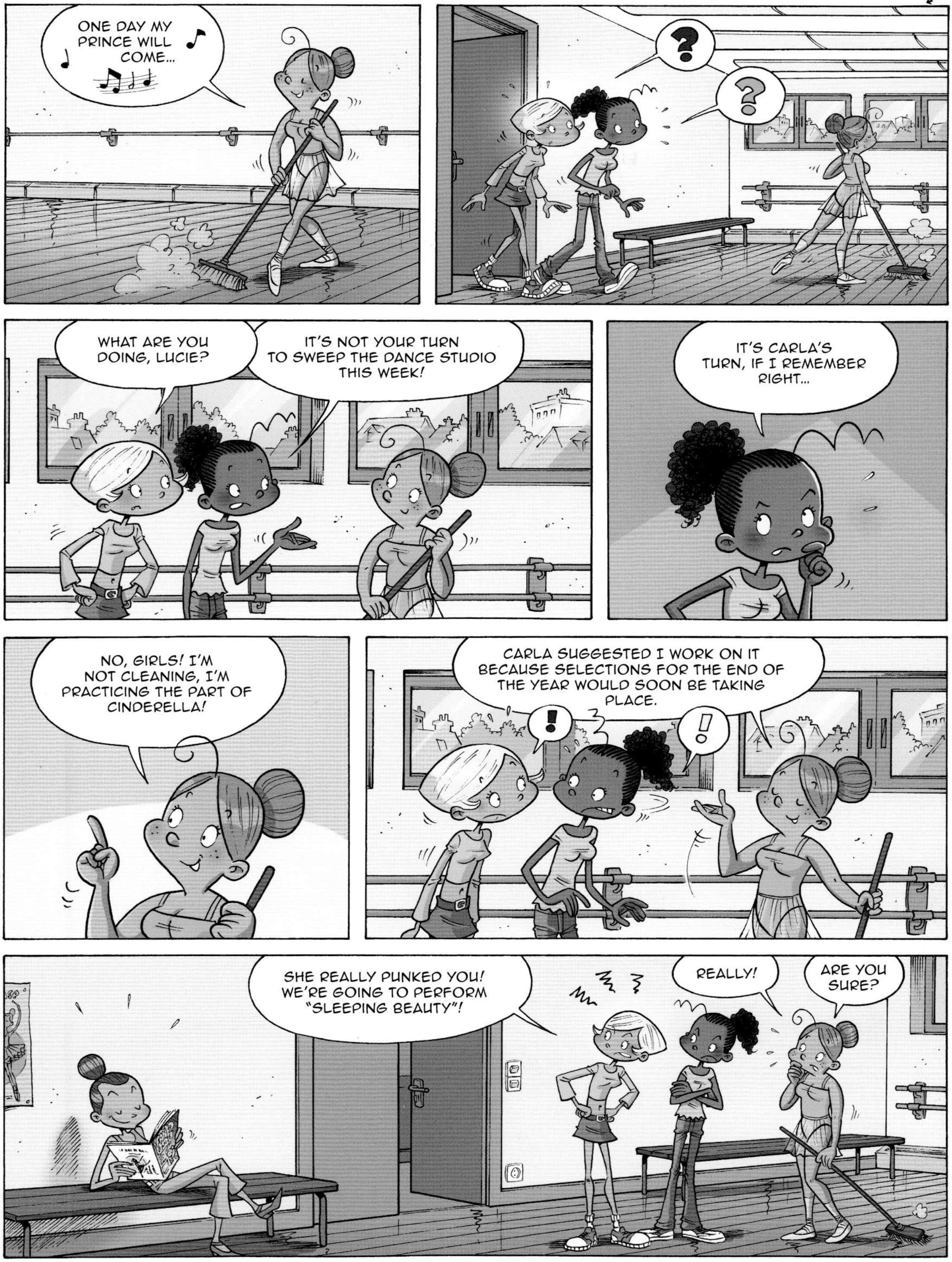
ONE DAY MY PRINCE WILL COME...
?
?
WHAT ARE YOU DOING, LUCIE?
IT'S NOT YOUR TURN TO SWEEP THE DANCE STUDIO THIS WEEK!
IT'S CARLA'S TURN, IF I REMEMBER RIGHT...
NO, GIRLS! I'M NOT CLEANING, I'M PRACTICING THE PART OF CINDERELLA!
CARLA SUGGESTED I WORK ON IT BECAUSE SELECTIONS FOR THE END OF THE YEAR WOULD SOON BE TAKING PLACE.
!
!
SHE REALLY PUNKED YOU! WE'RE GOING TO PERFORM "SLEEPING BEAUTY"!
REALLY!
ARE YOU SURE?

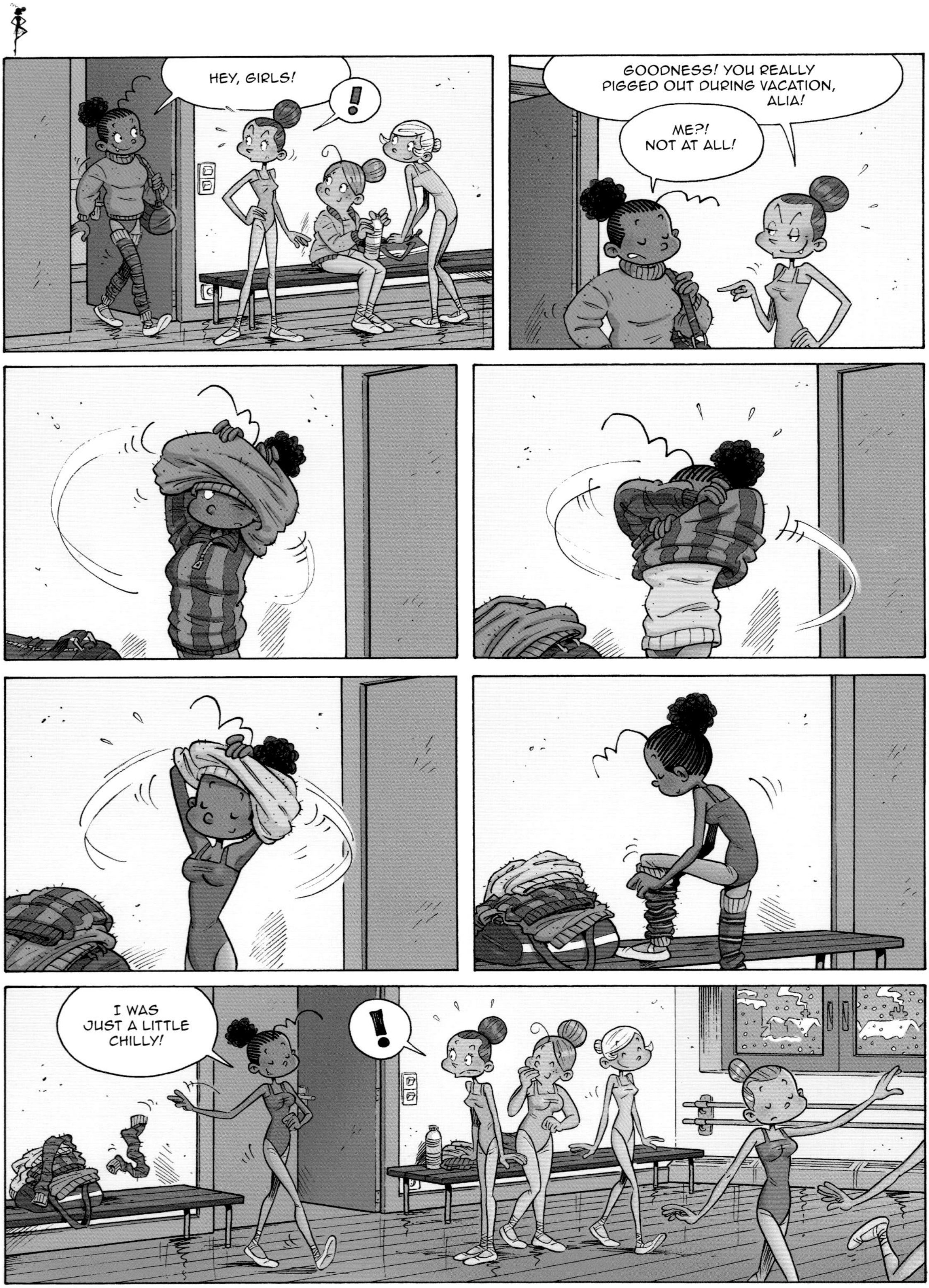
HEY, GIRLS!
!
GOODNESS! YOU REALLY PIGGED OUT DURING VACATION, ALIA!
ME?! NOT AT ALL!
I WAS JUST A LITTLE CHILLY!
!

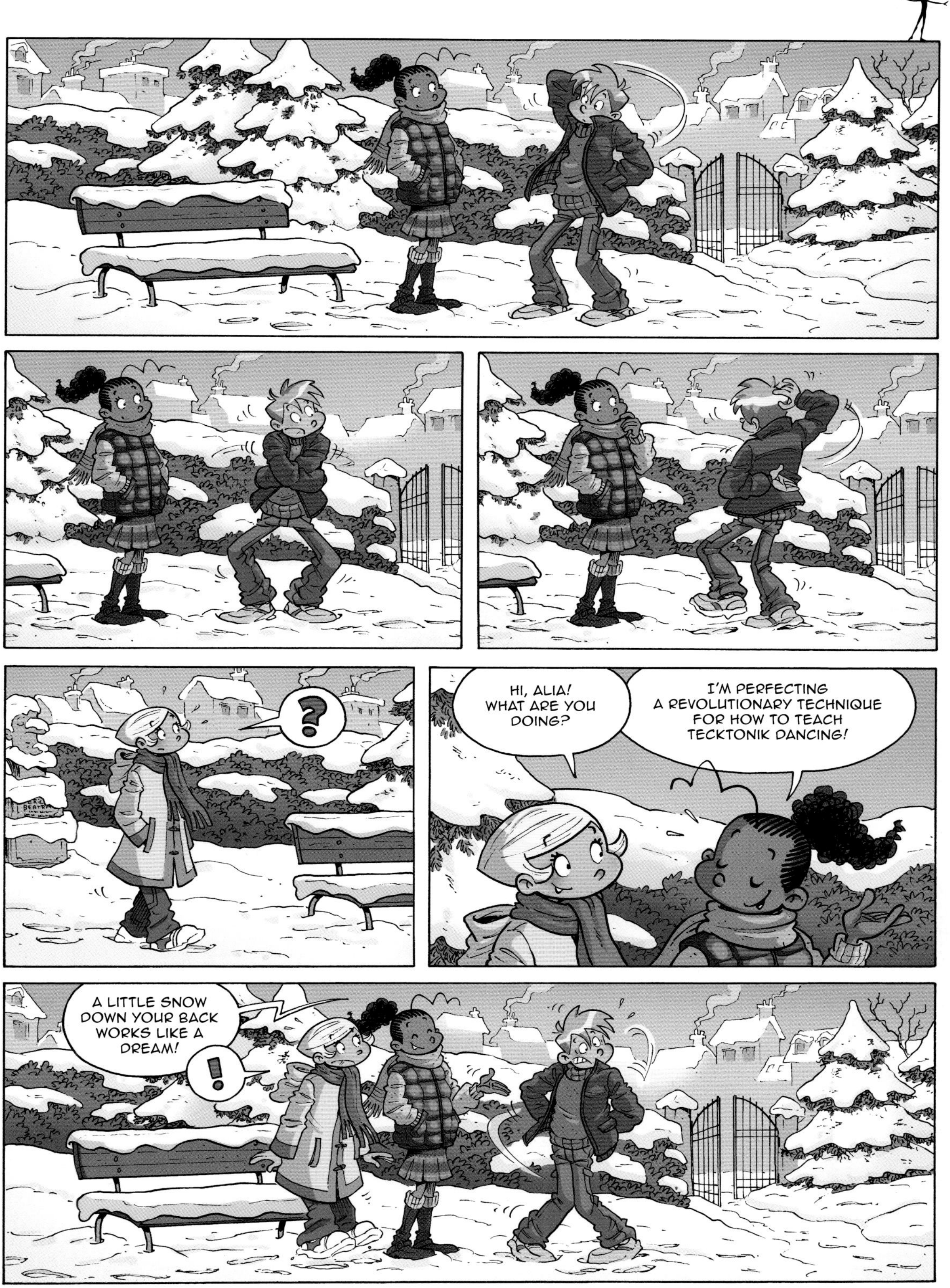
?
HI, ALIA! WHAT ARE YOU DOING?
I'M PERFECTING A REVOLUTIONARY TECHNIQUE FOR HOW TO TEACH TECKTONIK DANCING!
A LITTLE SNOW DOWN YOUR BACK WORKS LIKE A DREAM!
!

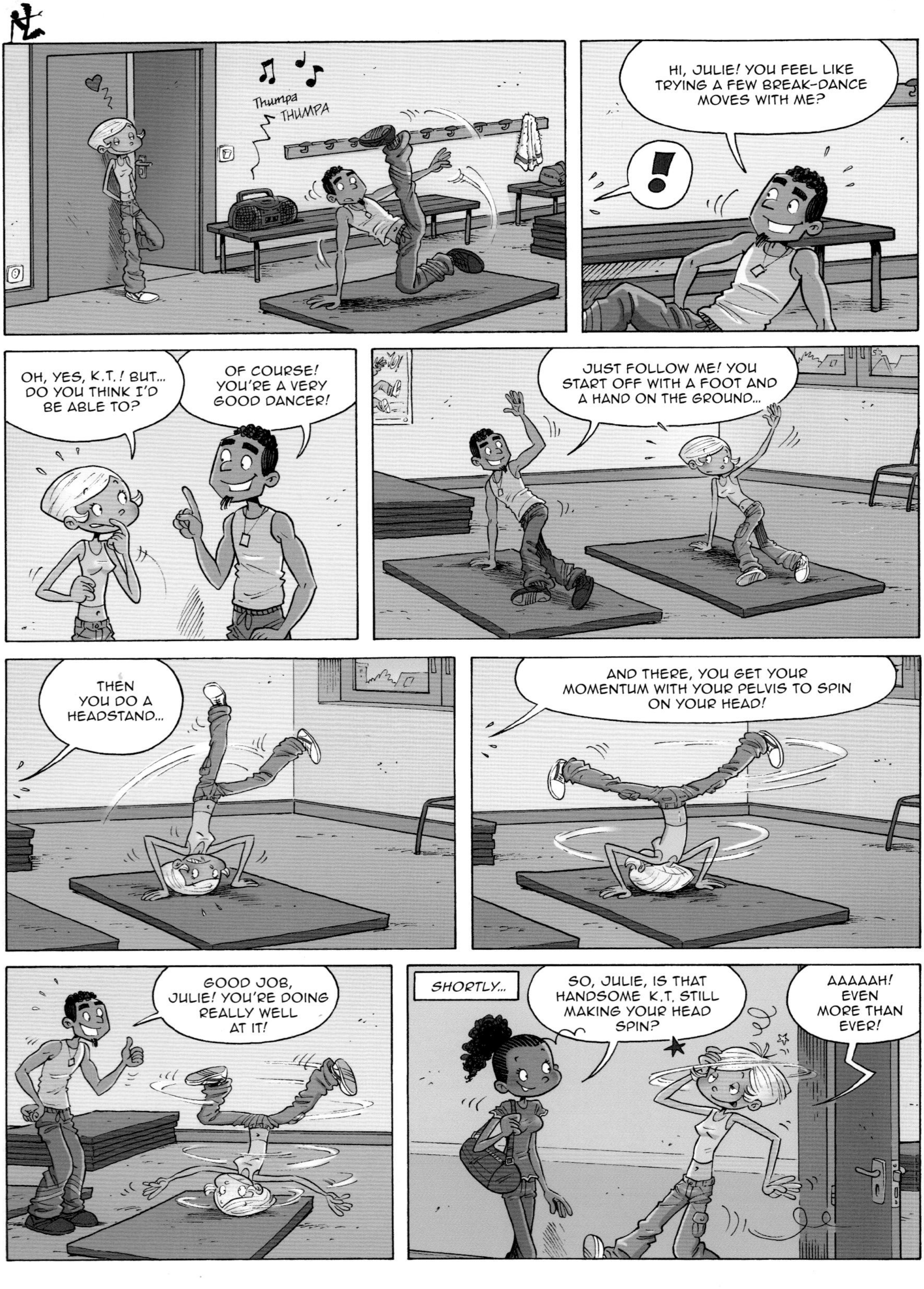
Thumpa
THUMPA
HI, JULIE! YOU FEEL LIKE TRYING A FEW BREAK-DANCE MOVES WITH ME?
!
OH, YES, K.T.! BUT... DO YOU THINK I'D BE ABLE TO?
OF COURSE! YOU'RE A VERY GOOD DANCER!
JUST FOLLOW ME! YOU START OFF WITH A FOOT AND A HAND ON THE GROUND...
THEN YOU DO A HEADSTAND...
AND THERE, YOU GET YOUR MOMENTUM WITH YOUR PELVIS TO SPIN ON YOUR HEAD!
GOOD JOB, JULIE! YOU'RE DOING REALLY WELL AT IT!
SHORTLY...
SO, JULIE, IS THAT HANDSOME K.T. STILL MAKING YOUR HEAD SPIN?
AAAAAH! EVEN MORE THAN EVER!

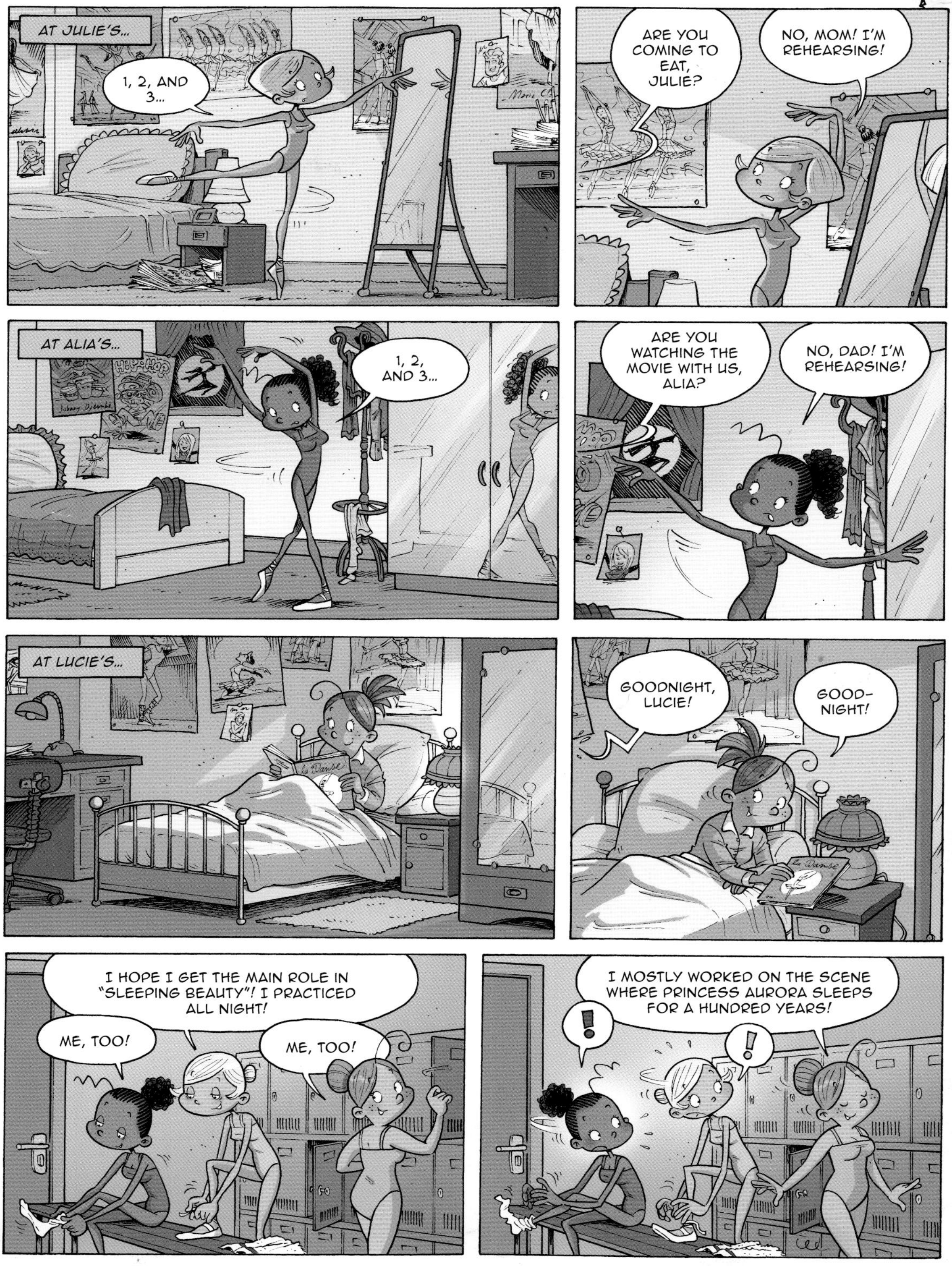
AT JULIE'S...
1, 2, AND 3...
ARE YOU COMING TO EAT, JULIE?
NO, MOM! I'M REHEARSING!
AT ALIA'S...
1, 2, AND 3...
ARE YOU WATCHING THE MOVIE WITH US, ALIA?
NO, DAD! I'M REHEARSING!
AT LUCIE'S...
GOODNIGHT, LUCIE!
GOOD-NIGHT!
I HOPE I GET THE MAIN ROLE IN "SLEEPING BEAUTY"! I PRACTICED ALL NIGHT!
ME, TOO!
ME, TOO!
I MOSTLY WORKED ON THE SCENE WHERE PRINCESS AURORA SLEEPS FOR A HUNDRED YEARS!
!
!

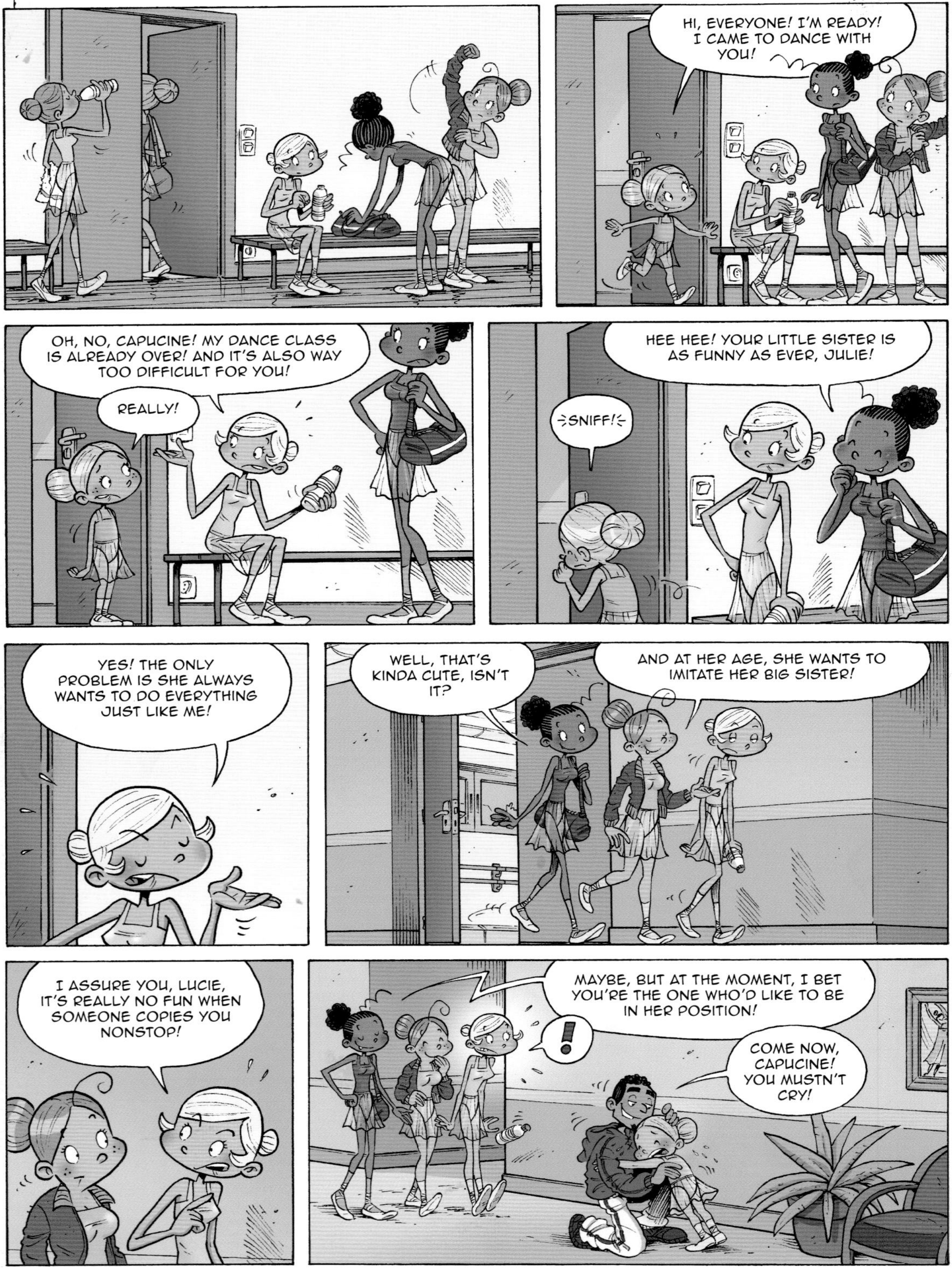

HI, EVERYONE! I'M READY! I CAME TO DANCE WITH YOU!
OH, NO, CAPUCINE! MY DANCE CLASS IS ALREADY OVER! AND IT'S ALSO WAY TOO DIFFICULT FOR YOU!
REALLY!
HEE HEE! YOUR LITTLE SISTER IS AS FUNNY AS EVER, JULIE!
SNIFF!
YES! THE ONLY PROBLEM IS SHE ALWAYS WANTS TO DO EVERYTHING JUST LIKE ME!
WELL, THAT'S KINDA CUTE, ISN'T IT?
AND AT HER AGE, SHE WANTS TO IMITATE HER BIG SISTER!
I ASSURE YOU, LUCIE, IT'S REALLY NO FUN WHEN SOMEONE COPIES YOU NONSTOP!
MAYBE, BUT AT THE MOMENT, I BET YOU'RE THE ONE WHO'D LIKE TO BE IN HER POSITION!
!
COME NOW, CAPUCINE! YOU MUSTN'T CRY!

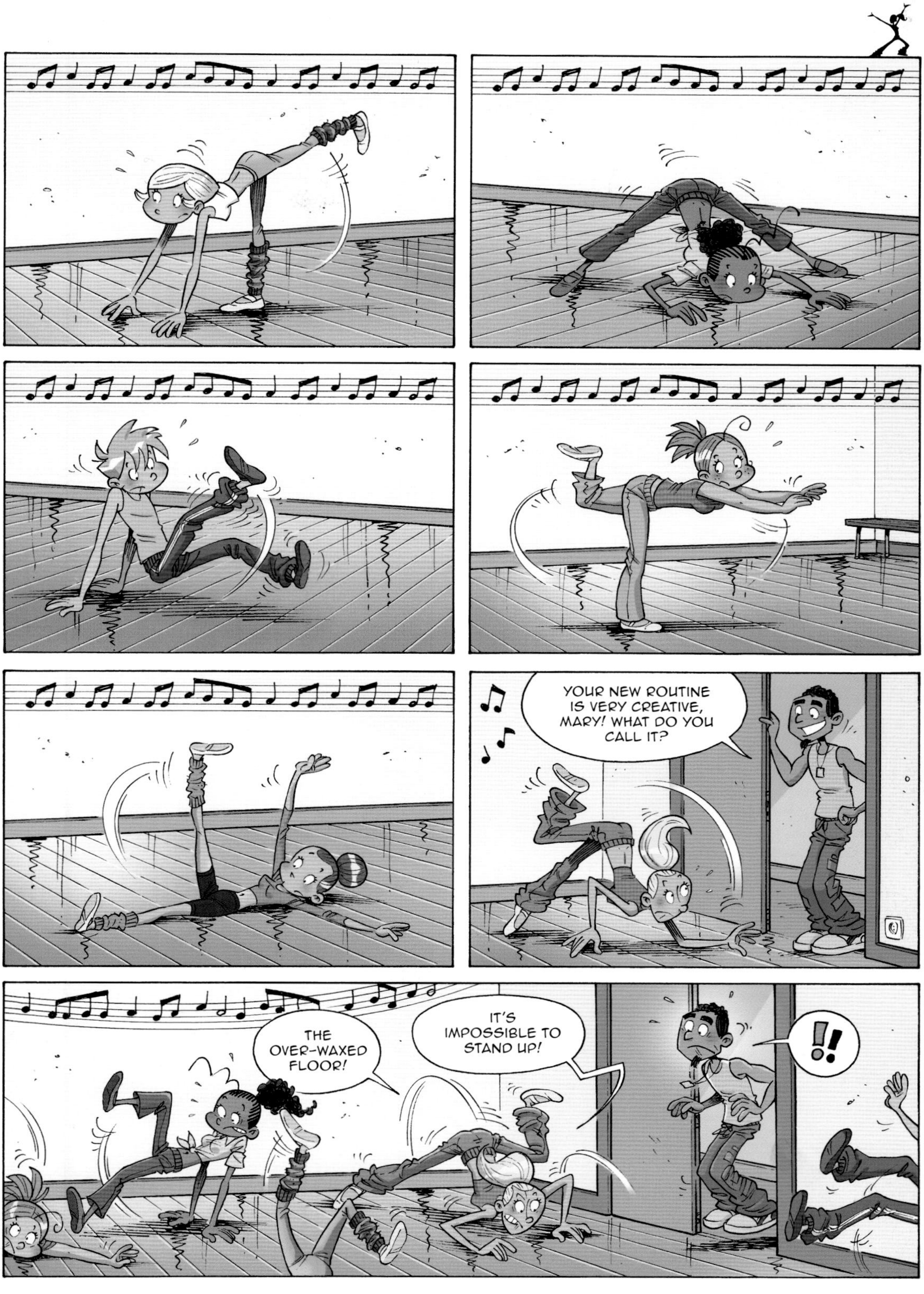
YOUR NEW ROUTINE IS VERY CREATIVE, MARY! WHAT DO YOU CALL IT?
THE OVER-WAXED FLOOR!
IT'S IMPOSSIBLE TO STAND UP!
!!

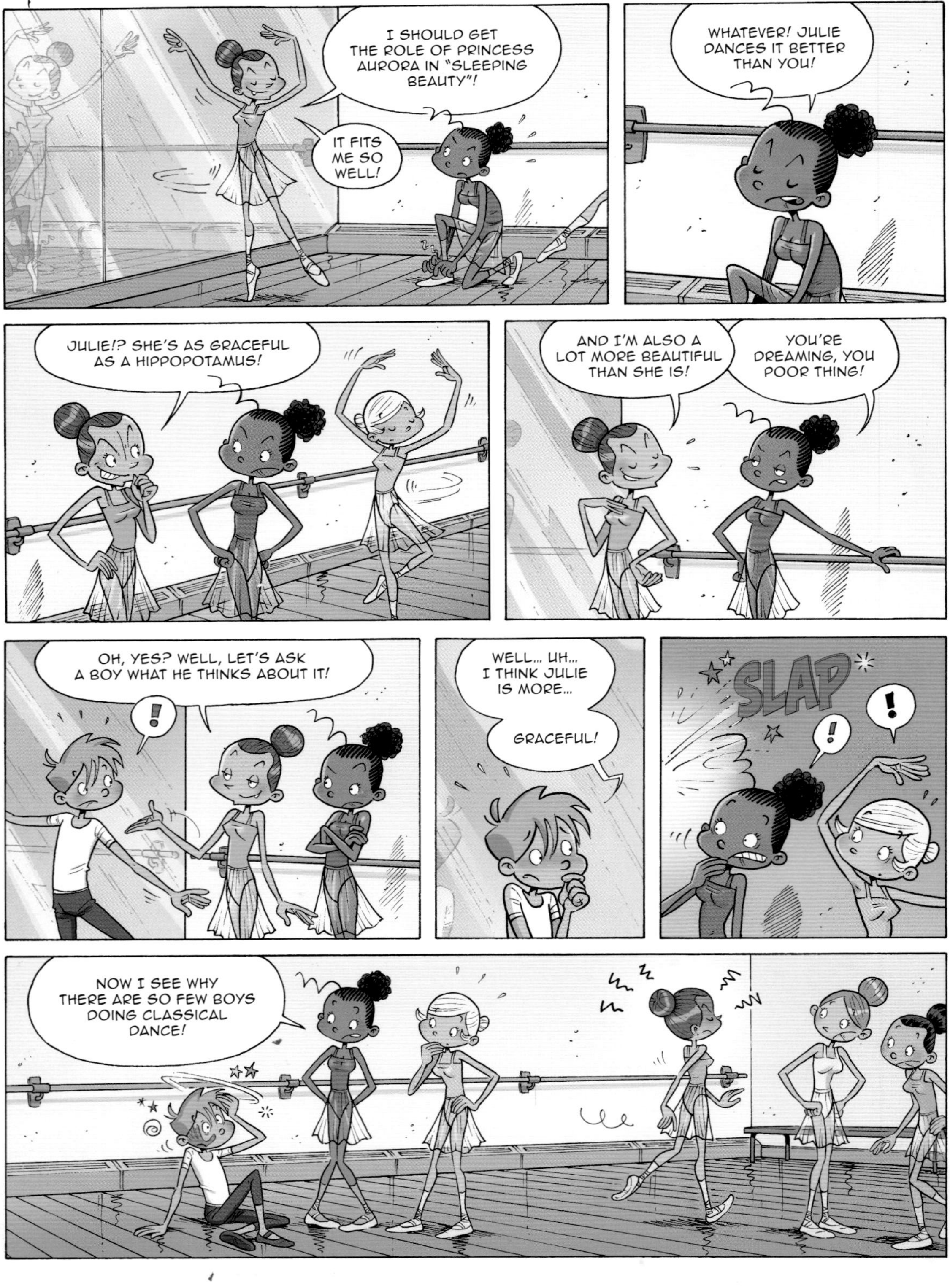
I SHOULD GET THE ROLE OF PRINCESS AURORA IN "SLEEPING BEAUTY"!
IT FITS ME SO WELL!
WHATEVER! JULIE DANCES IT BETTER THAN YOU!
JULIE!? SHE'S AS GRACEFUL AS A HIPPOPOTAMUS!
AND I'M ALSO A LOT MORE BEAUTIFUL THAN SHE IS!
YOU'RE DREAMING, YOU POOR THING!
OH, YES? WELL, LET'S ASK A BOY WHAT HE THINKS ABOUT IT!
!
WELL... UH... I THINK JULIE IS MORE...
GRACEFUL!
SLAP
!
!
NOW I SEE WHY THERE ARE SO FEW BOYS DOING CLASSICAL DANCE!

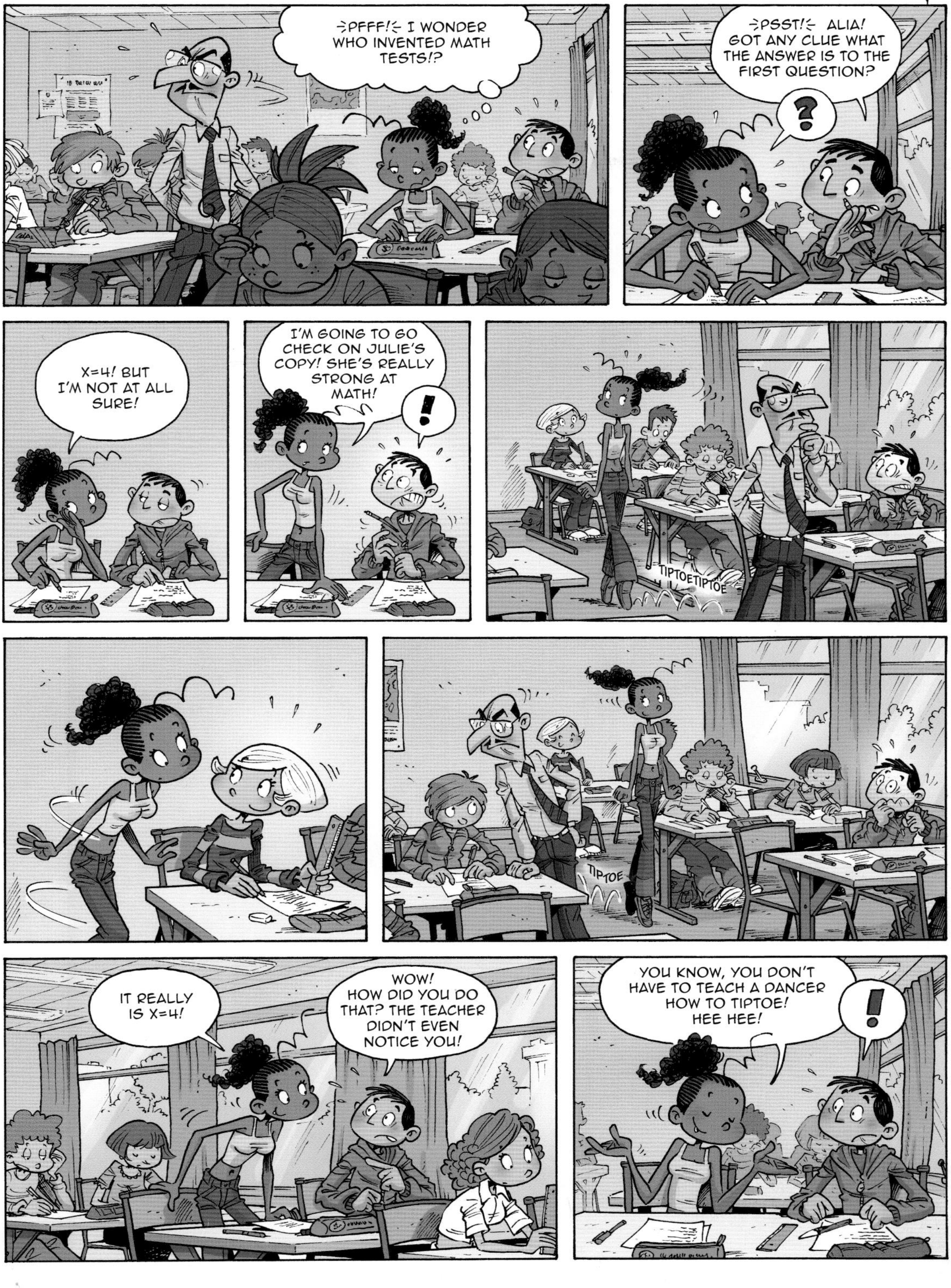
⇒PFFF!⇐ I WONDER WHO INVENTED MATH TESTS!?
⇒PSST!⇐ ALIA! GOT ANY CLUE WHAT THE ANSWER IS TO THE FIRST QUESTION?
?
X=4! BUT I'M NOT AT ALL SURE!
I'M GOING TO GO CHECK ON JULIE'S COPY! SHE'S REALLY STRONG AT MATH!
!
TIPTOETIPTOE
TIPTOE
IT REALLY IS X=4!
WOW! HOW DID YOU DO THAT? THE TEACHER DIDN'T EVEN NOTICE YOU!
YOU KNOW, YOU DON'T HAVE TO TEACH A DANCER HOW TO TIPTOE! HEE HEE!
!

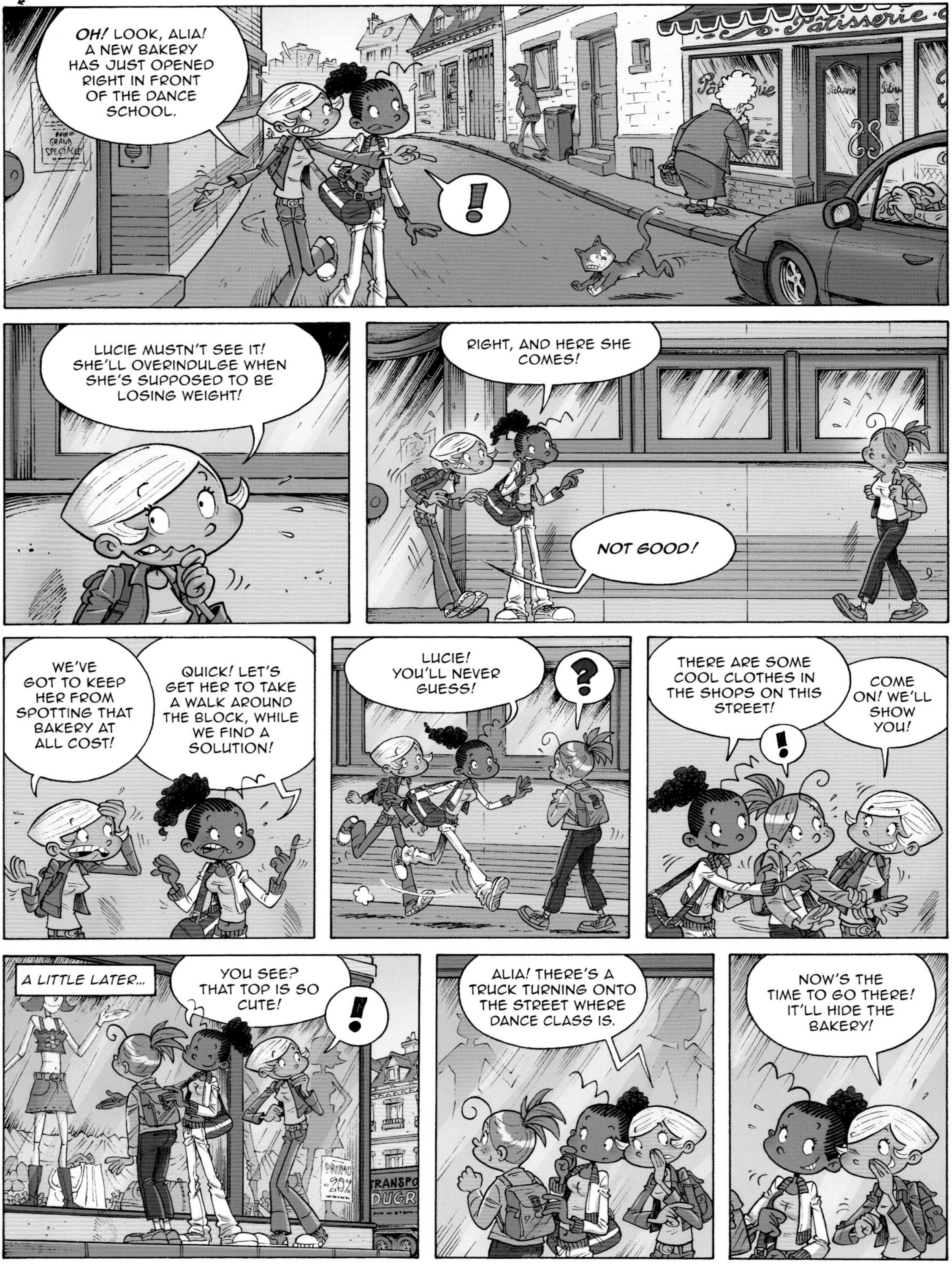
OH! LOOK, ALIA! A NEW BAKERY HAS JUST OPENED RIGHT IN FRONT OF THE DANCE SCHOOL.
!
Pâtisserie
LUCIE MUSTN'T SEE IT! SHE'LL OVERINDULGE WHEN SHE'S SUPPOSED TO BE LOSING WEIGHT!
RIGHT, AND HERE SHE COMES!
NOT GOOD!
WE'VE GOT TO KEEP HER FROM SPOTTING THAT BAKERY AT ALL COST!
QUICK! LET'S GET HER TO TAKE A WALK AROUND THE BLOCK, WHILE WE FIND A SOLUTION!
LUCIE! YOU'LL NEVER GUESS!
?
THERE ARE SOME COOL CLOTHES IN THE SHOPS ON THIS STREET!
!
COME ON! WE'LL SHOW YOU!
A LITTLE LATER...
YOU SEE? THAT TOP IS SO CUTE!
!
PROMO -20%
ALIA! THERE'S A TRUCK TURNING ONTO THE STREET WHERE DANCE CLASS IS.
NOW'S THE TIME TO GO THERE! IT'LL HIDE THE BAKERY!

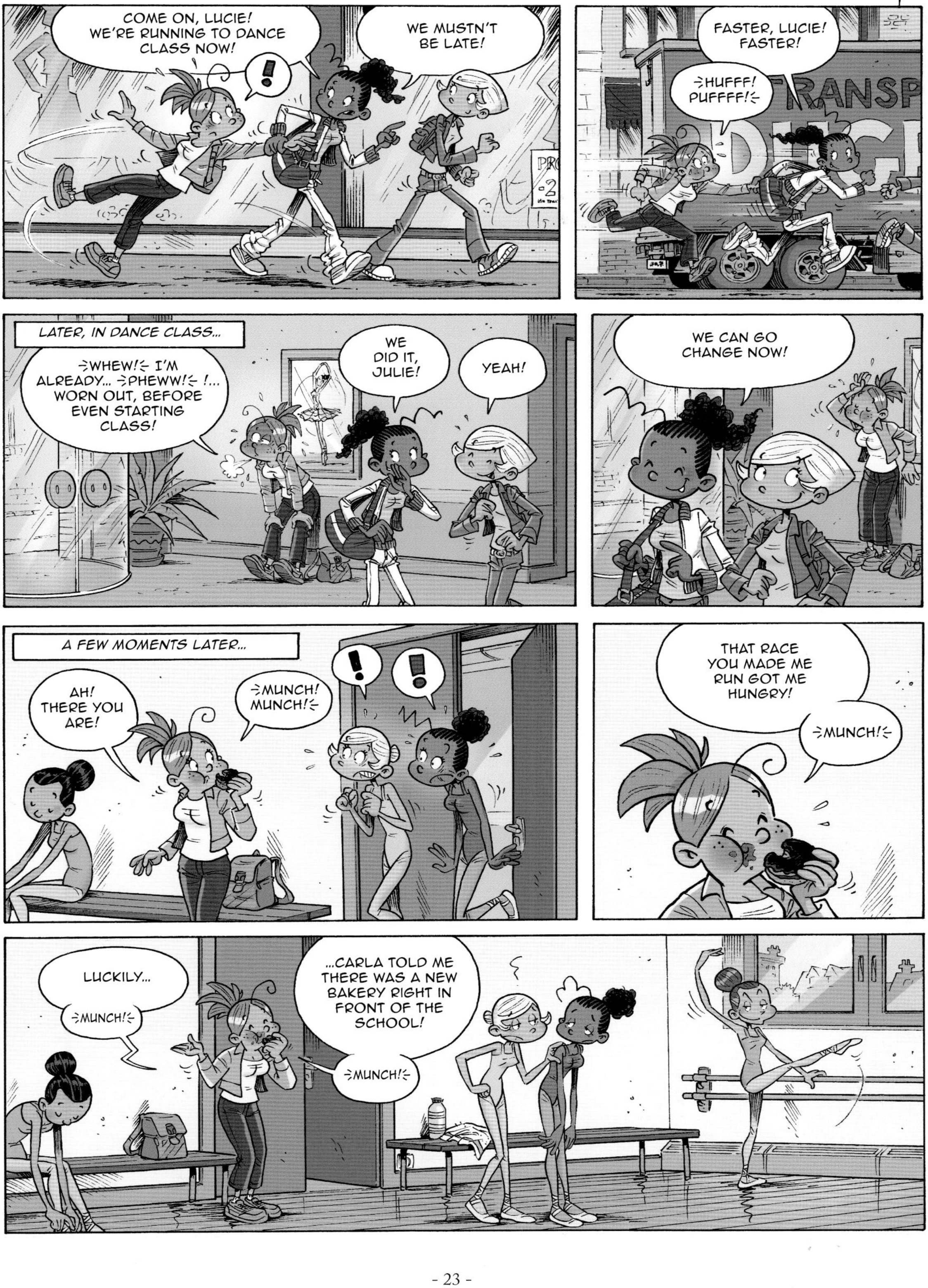
COME ON, LUCIE! WE'RE RUNNING TO DANCE CLASS NOW!
!
WE MUSTN'T BE LATE!
FASTER, LUCIE! FASTER!
HUFFF! PUFFFF!
LATER, IN DANCE CLASS...
WHEW! I'M ALREADY... PHEWW! !... WORN OUT, BEFORE EVEN STARTING CLASS!
WE DID IT, JULIE!
YEAH!
WE CAN GO CHANGE NOW!
A FEW MOMENTS LATER...
AH! THERE YOU ARE!
MUNCH! MUNCH!
!
!
THAT RACE YOU MADE ME RUN GOT ME HUNGRY!
MUNCH!
LUCKILY...
MUNCH!
...CARLA TOLD ME THERE WAS A NEW BAKERY RIGHT IN FRONT OF THE SCHOOL!
MUNCH!

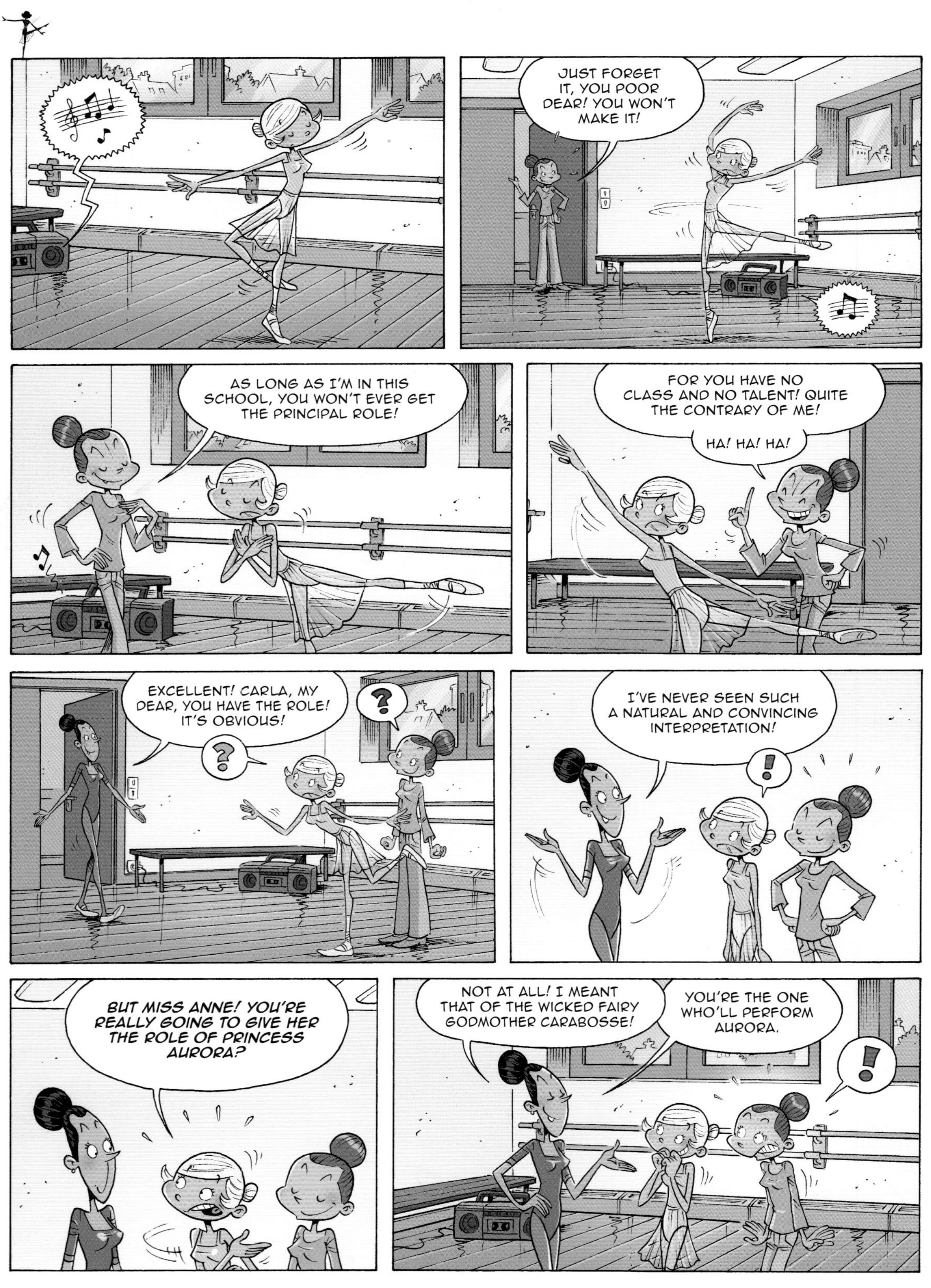

JUST FORGET IT, YOU POOR DEAR! YOU WON'T MAKE IT!
AS LONG AS I'M IN THIS SCHOOL, YOU WON'T EVER GET THE PRINCIPAL ROLE!
FOR YOU HAVE NO CLASS AND NO TALENT! QUITE THE CONTRARY OF ME!
HA! HA! HA!
EXCELLENT! CARLA, MY DEAR, YOU HAVE THE ROLE! IT'S OBVIOUS!
?
?
I'VE NEVER SEEN SUCH A NATURAL AND CONVINCING INTERPRETATION!
!
BUT MISS ANNE! YOU'RE REALLY GOING TO GIVE HER THE ROLE OF PRINCESS AURORA?
NOT AT ALL! I MEANT THAT OF THE WICKED FAIRY GODMOTHER CARABOSSE!
YOU'RE THE ONE WHO'LL PERFORM AURORA.
!

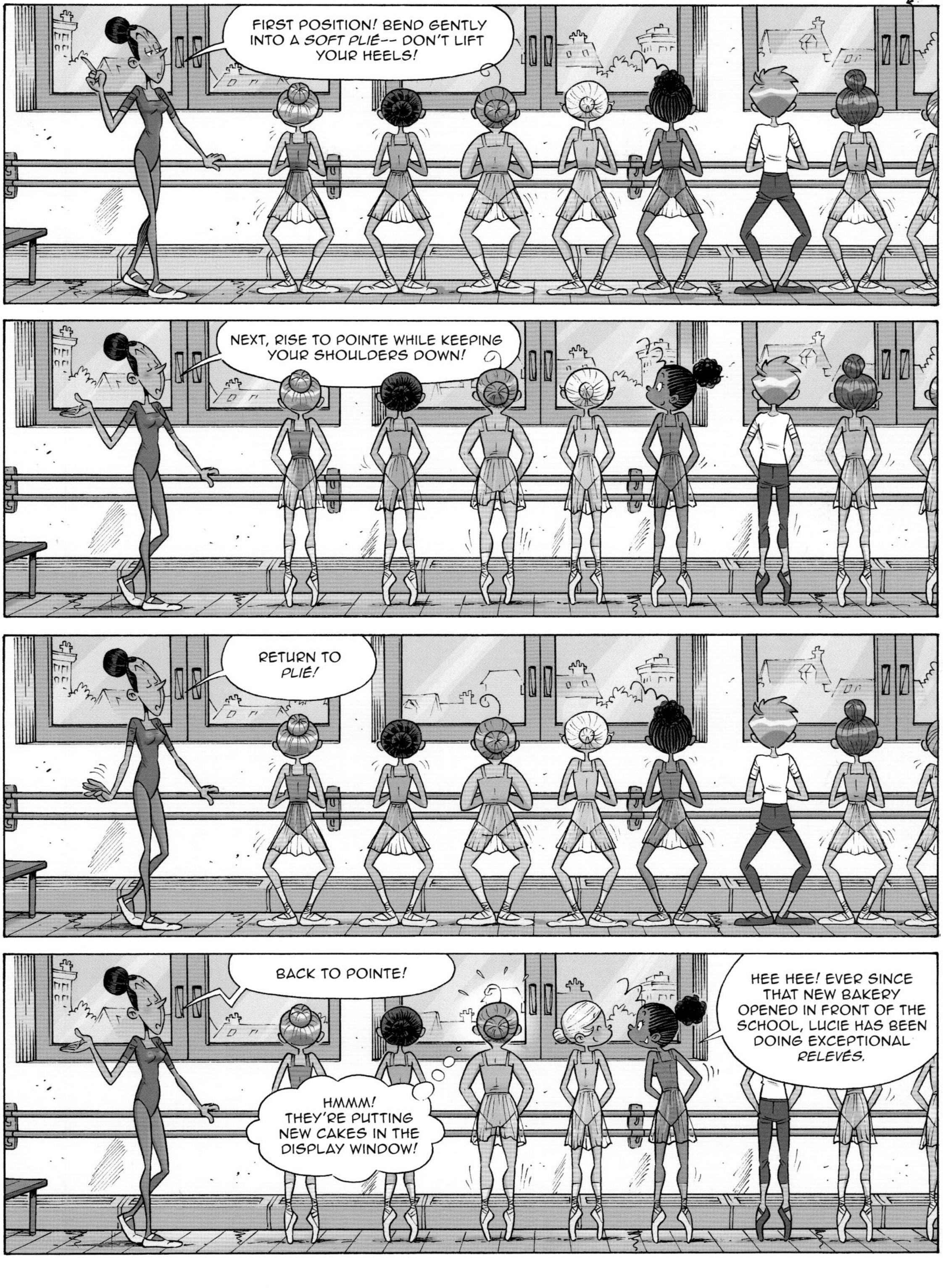
FIRST POSITION! BEND GENTLY INTO A *SOFT PLIÉ*-- DON'T LIFT YOUR HEELS!
NEXT, RISE TO POINTE WHILE KEEPING YOUR SHOULDERS DOWN!
RETURN TO *PLIÉ!*
BACK TO POINTE!
HMMM! THEY'RE PUTTING NEW CAKES IN THE DISPLAY WINDOW!
HEE HEE! EVER SINCE THAT NEW BAKERY OPENED IN FRONT OF THE SCHOOL, LUCIE HAS BEEN DOING EXCEPTIONAL *RELEVÉS.*

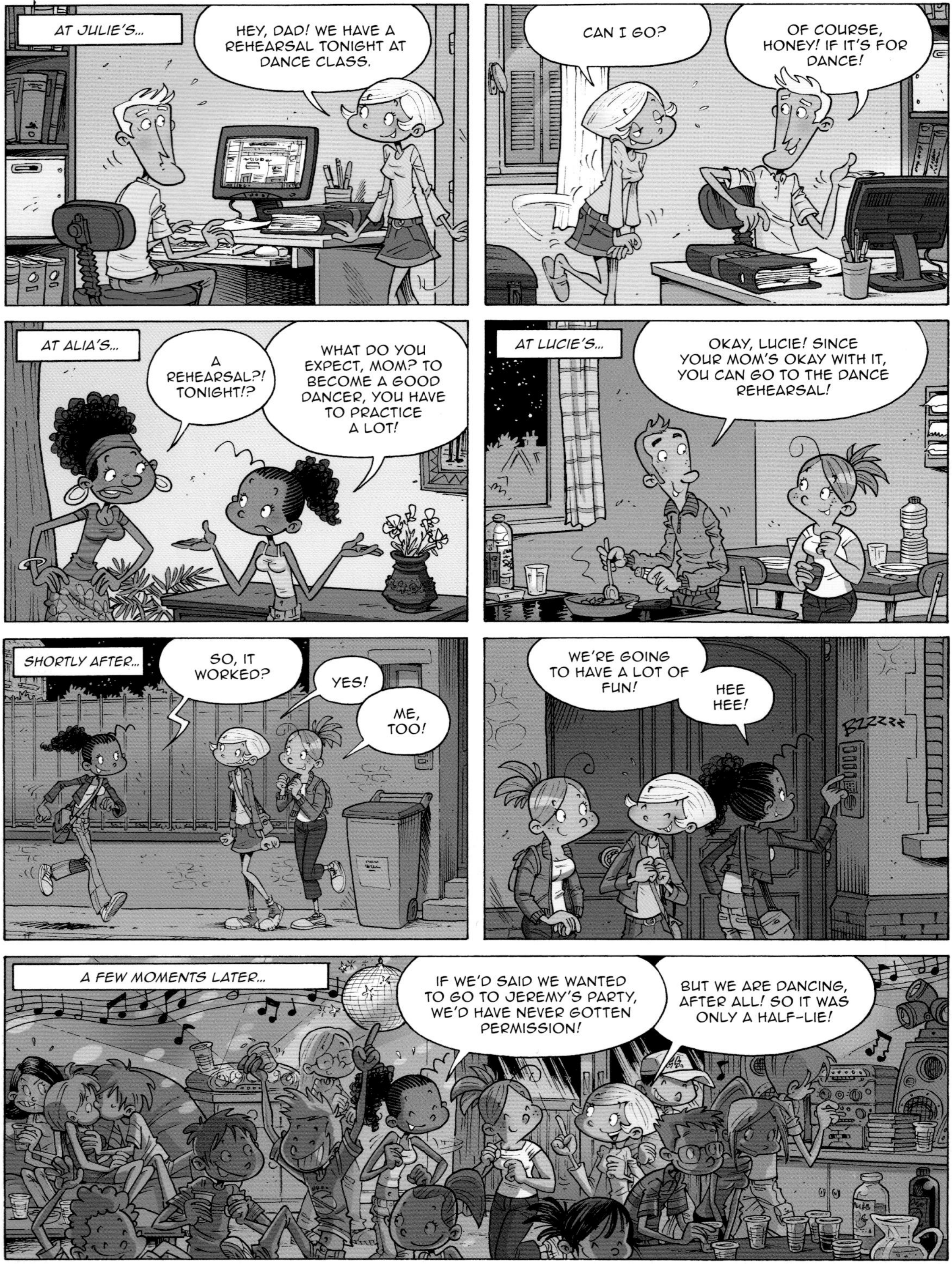
AT JULIE'S...
HEY, DAD! WE HAVE A REHEARSAL TONIGHT AT DANCE CLASS.
CAN I GO?
OF COURSE, HONEY! IF IT'S FOR DANCE!
AT ALIA'S...
A REHEARSAL?! TONIGHT!?
WHAT DO YOU EXPECT, MOM? TO BECOME A GOOD DANCER, YOU HAVE TO PRACTICE A LOT!
AT LUCIE'S...
OKAY, LUCIE! SINCE YOUR MOM'S OKAY WITH IT, YOU CAN GO TO THE DANCE REHEARSAL!
SHORTLY AFTER...
SO, IT WORKED?
YES!
ME, TOO!
WE'RE GOING TO HAVE A LOT OF FUN!
HEE HEE!
BZZZZZ
A FEW MOMENTS LATER...
IF WE'D SAID WE WANTED TO GO TO JEREMY'S PARTY, WE'D HAVE NEVER GOTTEN PERMISSION!
BUT WE ARE DANCING, AFTER ALL! SO IT WAS ONLY A HALF-LIE!

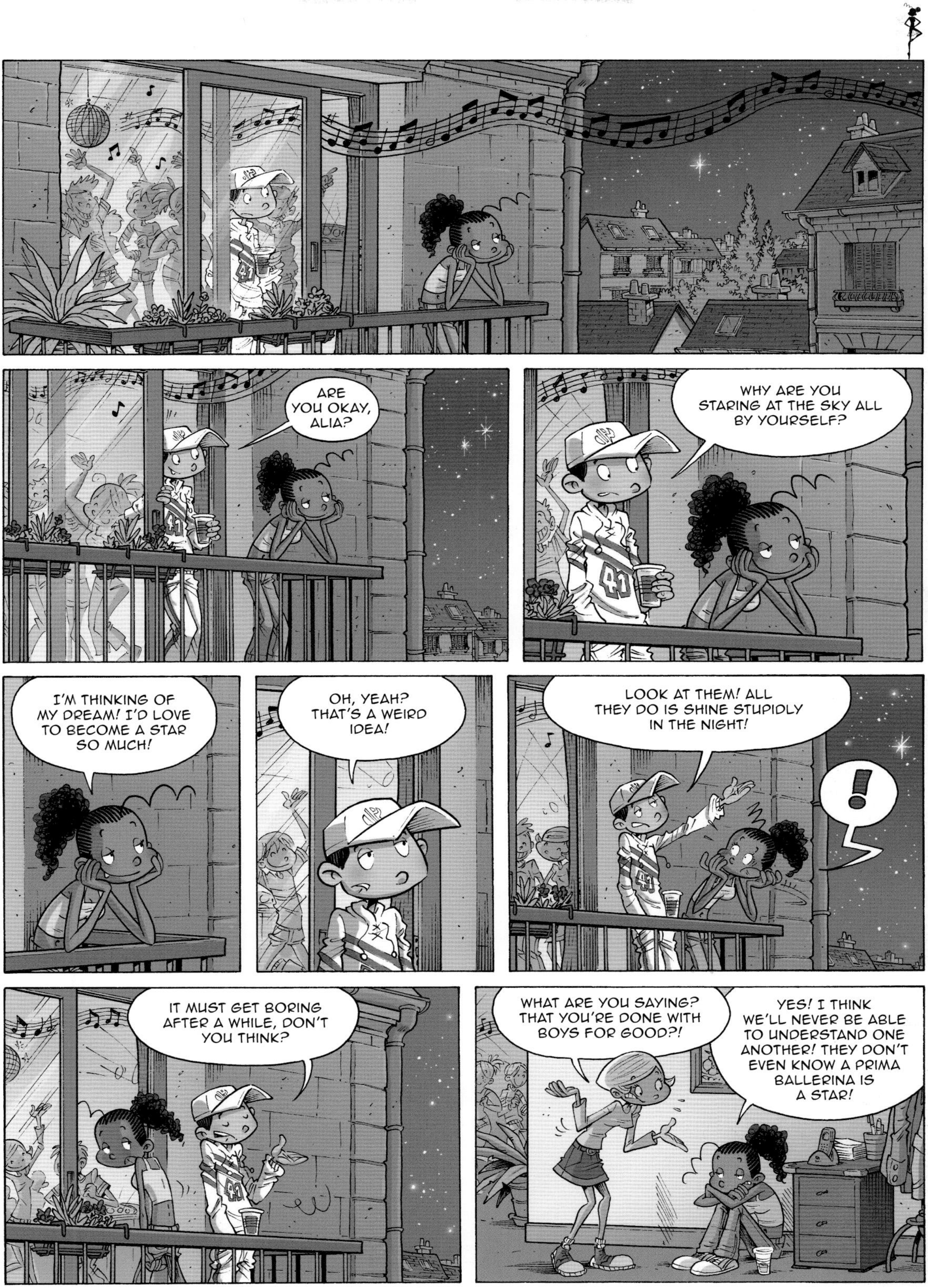
ARE YOU OKAY, ALIA?
WHY ARE YOU STARING AT THE SKY ALL BY YOURSELF?
I'M THINKING OF MY DREAM! I'D LOVE TO BECOME A STAR SO MUCH!
OH, YEAH? THAT'S A WEIRD IDEA!
LOOK AT THEM! ALL THEY DO IS SHINE STUPIDLY IN THE NIGHT!
!
IT MUST GET BORING AFTER A WHILE, DON'T YOU THINK?
WHAT ARE YOU SAYING? THAT YOU'RE DONE WITH BOYS FOR GOOD?!
YES! I THINK WE'LL NEVER BE ABLE TO UNDERSTAND ONE ANOTHER! THEY DON'T EVEN KNOW A PRIMA BALLERINA IS A STAR!

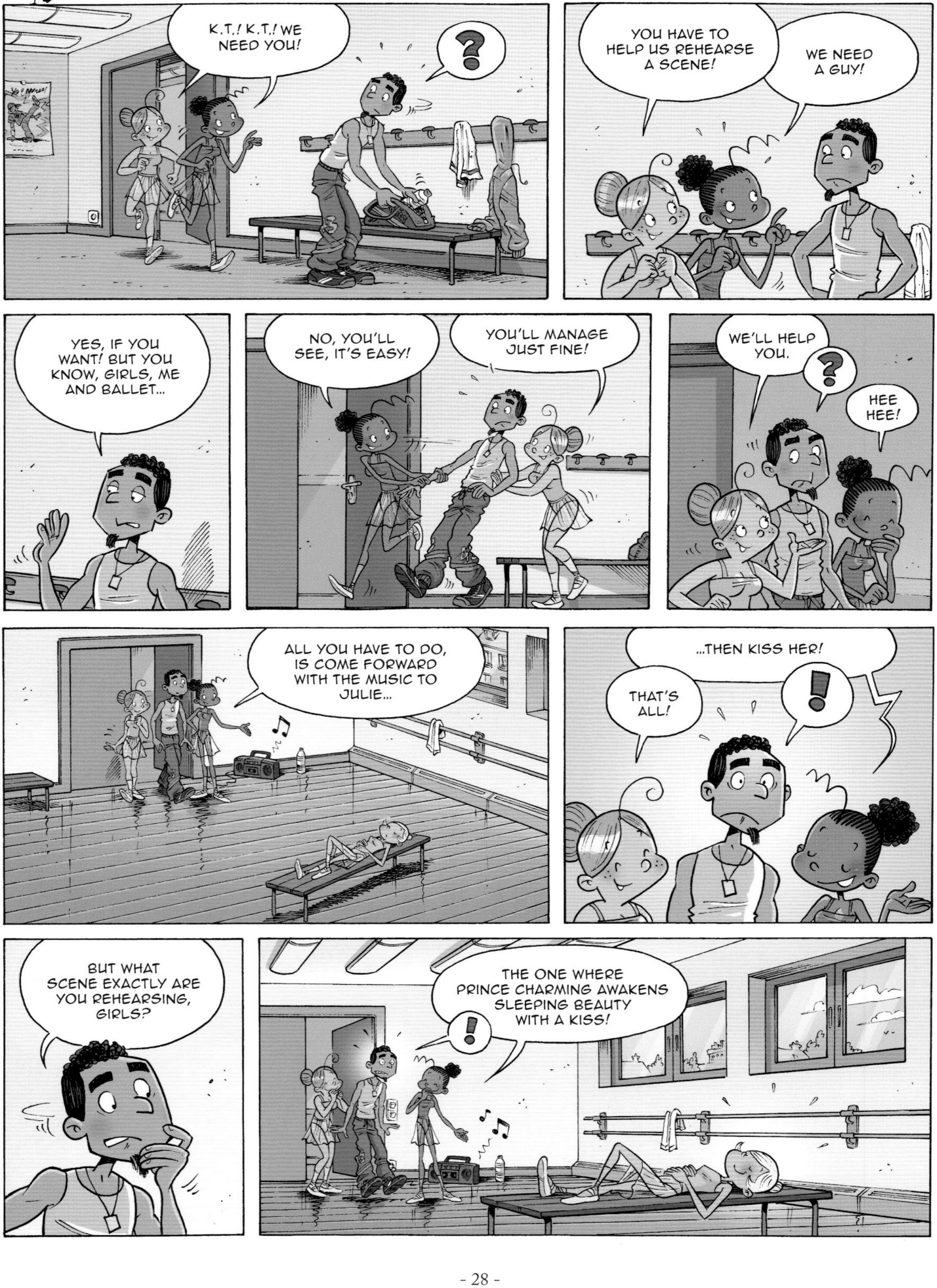
K.T.! K.T.! WE NEED YOU!
?
YOU HAVE TO HELP US REHEARSE A SCENE!
WE NEED A GUY!
YES, IF YOU WANT! BUT YOU KNOW, GIRLS, ME AND BALLET...
NO, YOU'LL SEE, IT'S EASY!
YOU'LL MANAGE JUST FINE!
WE'LL HELP YOU.
?
HEE HEE!
ALL YOU HAVE TO DO, IS COME FORWARD WITH THE MUSIC TO JULIE...
THAT'S ALL!
...THEN KISS HER!
!
BUT WHAT SCENE EXACTLY ARE YOU REHEARSING, GIRLS?
!
THE ONE WHERE PRINCE CHARMING AWAKENS SLEEPING BEAUTY WITH A KISS!

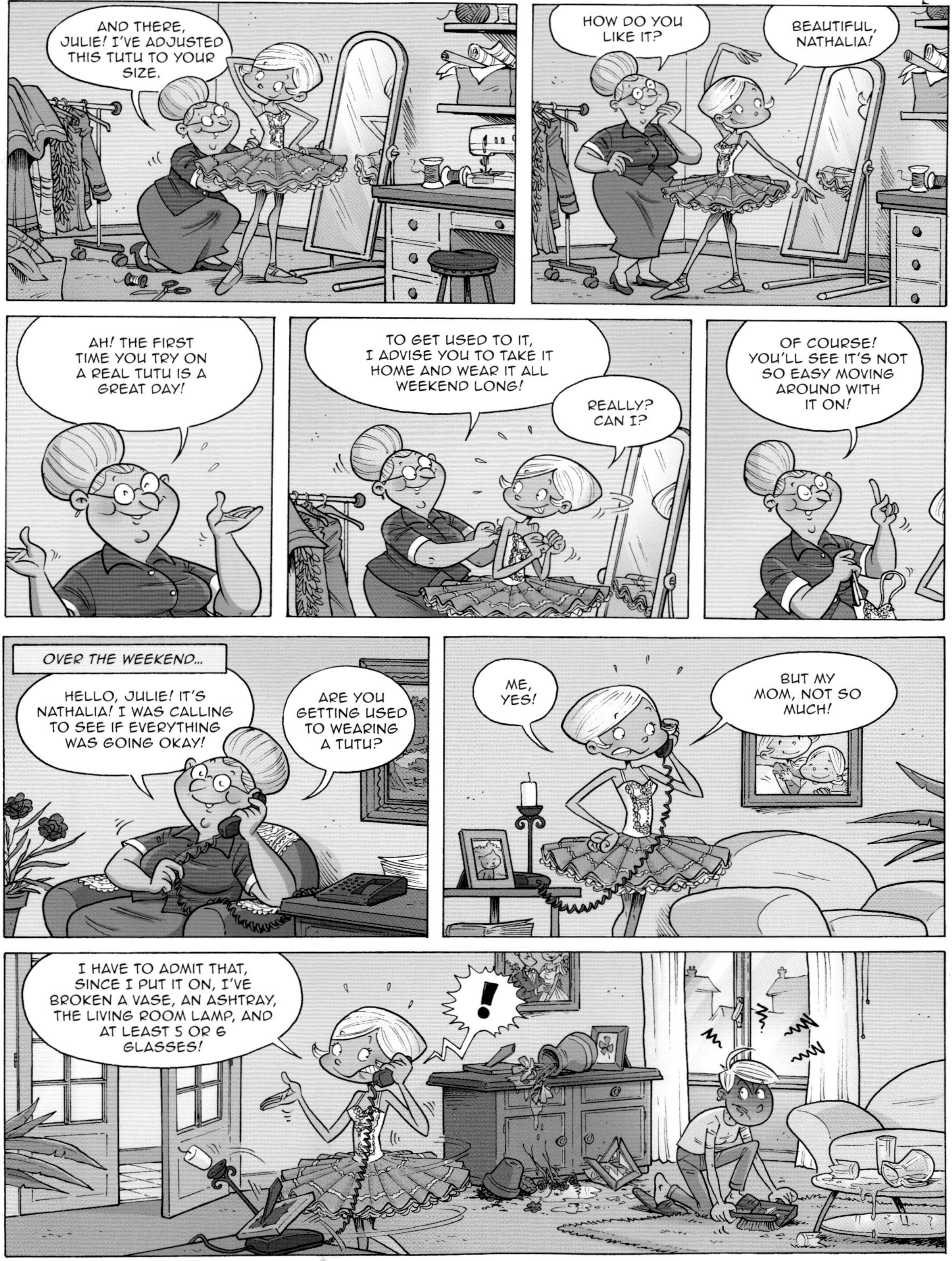
AND THERE, JULIE! I'VE ADJUSTED THIS TUTU TO YOUR SIZE.
HOW DO YOU LIKE IT?
BEAUTIFUL, NATHALIA!
AH! THE FIRST TIME YOU TRY ON A REAL TUTU IS A GREAT DAY!
TO GET USED TO IT, I ADVISE YOU TO TAKE IT HOME AND WEAR IT ALL WEEKEND LONG!
REALLY? CAN I?
OF COURSE! YOU'LL SEE IT'S NOT SO EASY MOVING AROUND WITH IT ON!
OVER THE WEEKEND...
HELLO, JULIE! IT'S NATHALIA! I WAS CALLING TO SEE IF EVERYTHING WAS GOING OKAY!
ARE YOU GETTING USED TO WEARING A TUTU?
ME, YES!
BUT MY MOM, NOT SO MUCH!
I HAVE TO ADMIT THAT, SINCE I PUT IT ON, I'VE BROKEN A VASE, AN ASHTRAY, THE LIVING ROOM LAMP, AND AT LEAST 5 OR 6 GLASSES!
!

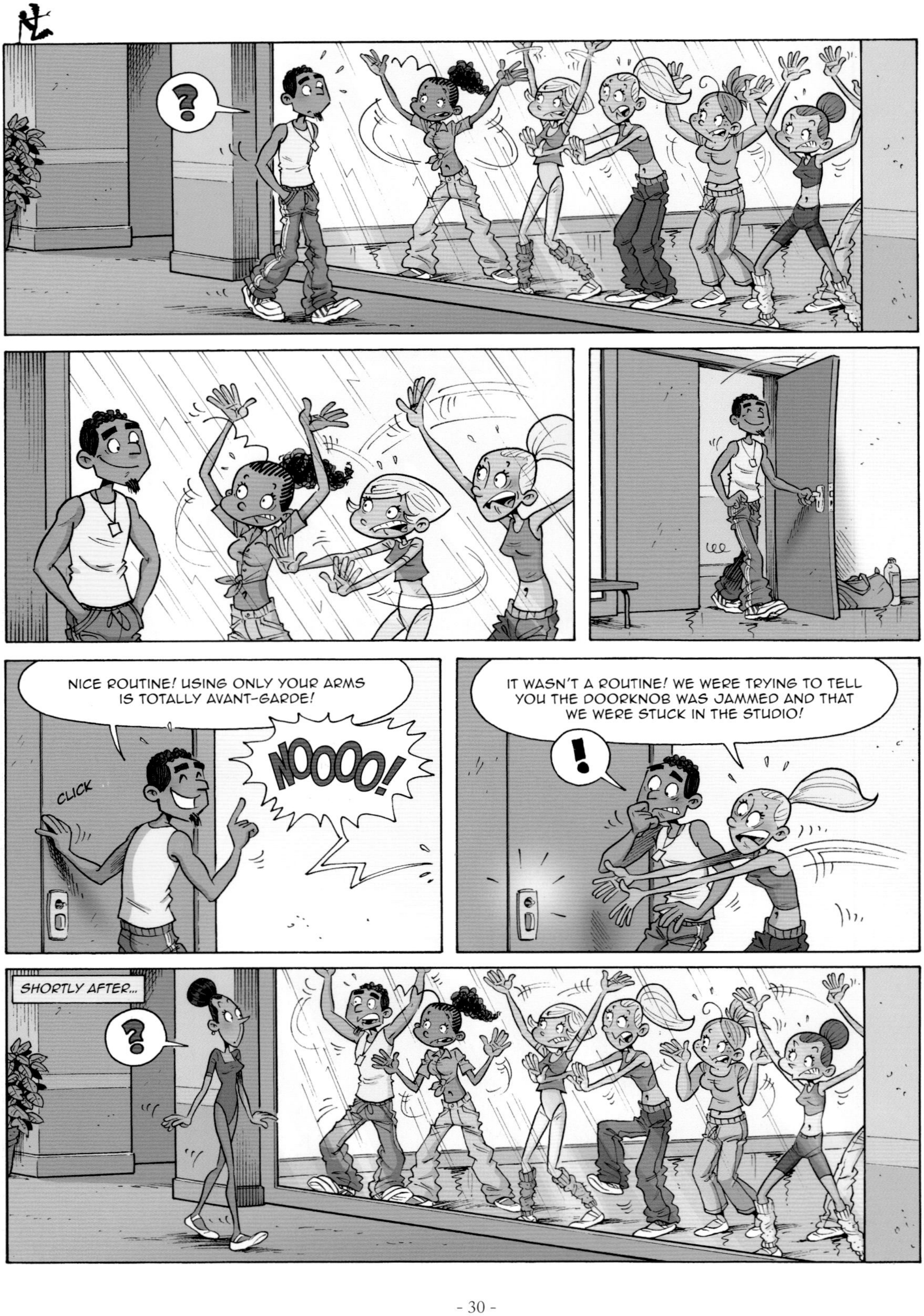
?
NICE ROUTINE! USING ONLY YOUR ARMS IS TOTALLY AVANT-GARDE!
CLICK
NOOOO!
IT WASN'T A ROUTINE! WE WERE TRYING TO TELL YOU THE DOORKNOB WAS JAMMED AND THAT WE WERE STUCK IN THE STUDIO!
!
SHORTLY AFTER...
?

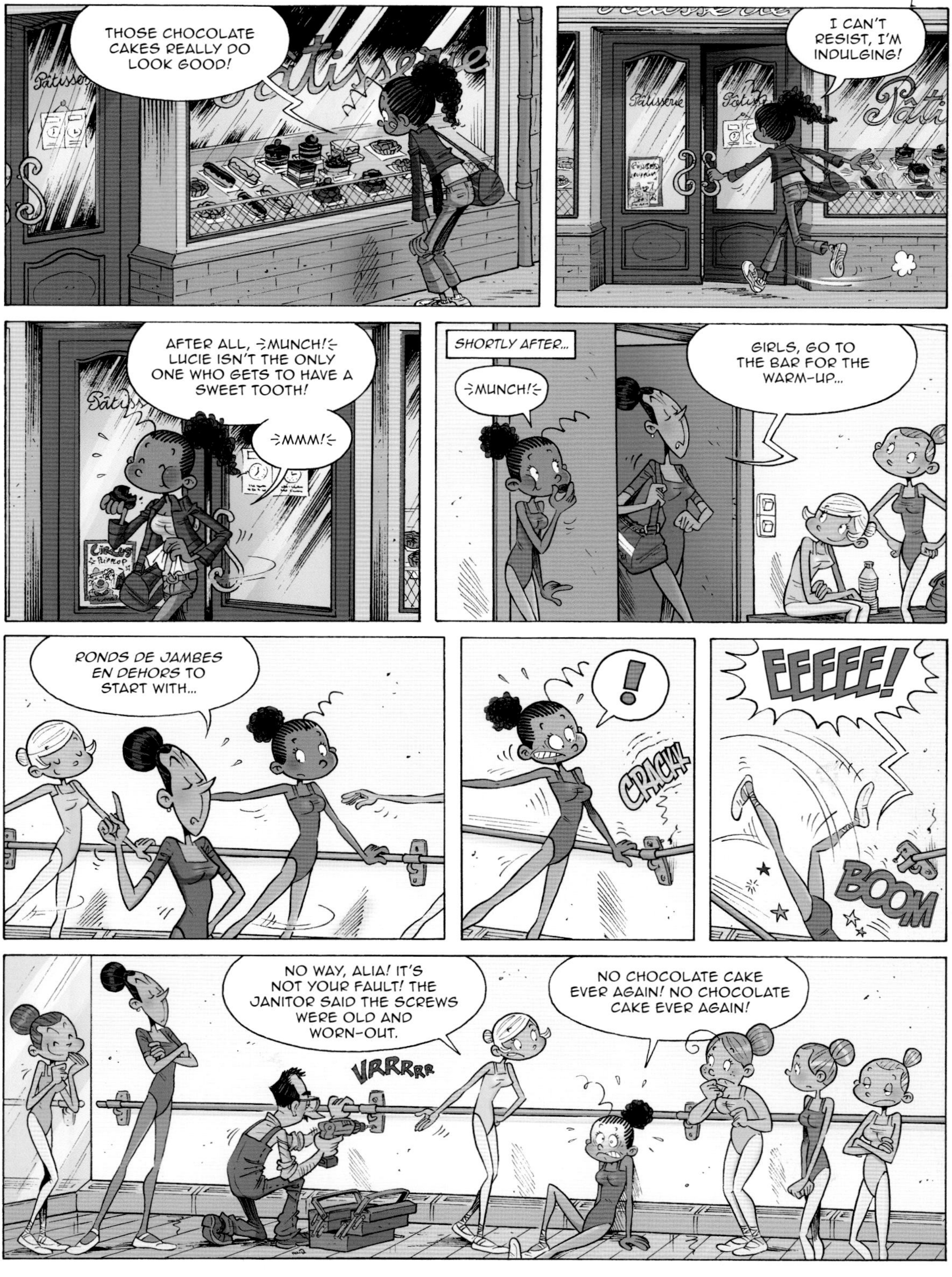
THOSE CHOCOLATE CAKES REALLY DO LOOK GOOD!
Pâtisserie
I CAN'T RESIST, I'M INDULGING!
AFTER ALL, ⋛MUNCH!⋚ LUCIE ISN'T THE ONLY ONE WHO GETS TO HAVE A SWEET TOOTH!
⋛MMM!⋚
SHORTLY AFTER...
⋛MUNCH!⋚
GIRLS, GO TO THE BAR FOR THE WARM-UP...
RONDS DE JAMBES EN DEHORS TO START WITH...
!
CRACK!
EEEEE!
BOOM
NO WAY, ALIA! IT'S NOT YOUR FAULT! THE JANITOR SAID THE SCREWS WERE OLD AND WORN-OUT.
VRRRRR
NO CHOCOLATE CAKE EVER AGAIN! NO CHOCOLATE CAKE EVER AGAIN!

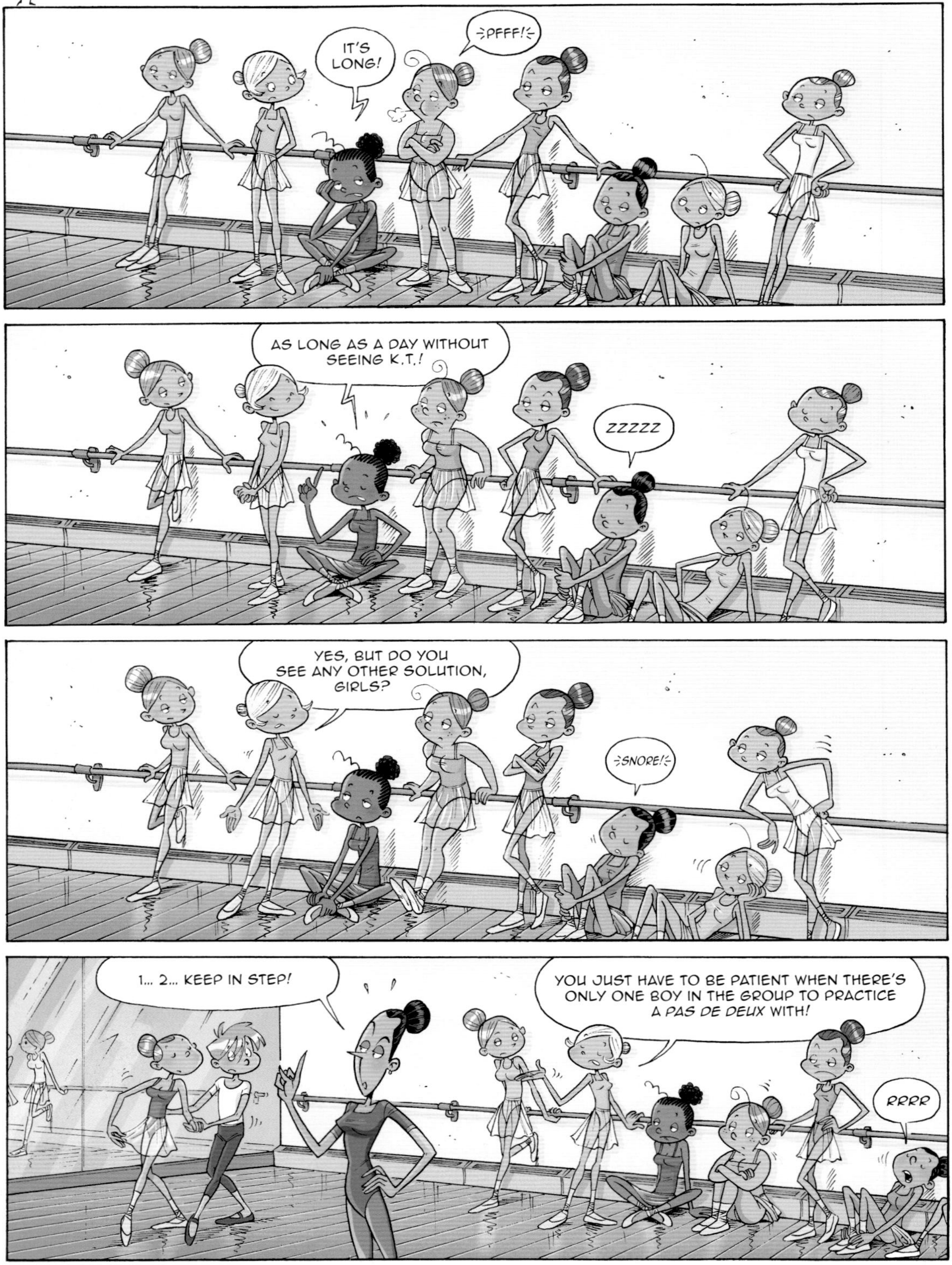

IT'S LONG!
PFFF!
AS LONG AS A DAY WITHOUT SEEING K.T.!
ZZZZZ
YES, BUT DO YOU SEE ANY OTHER SOLUTION, GIRLS?
SNORE!
1... 2... KEEP IN STEP!
YOU JUST HAVE TO BE PATIENT WHEN THERE'S ONLY ONE BOY IN THE GROUP TO PRACTICE A *PAS DE DEUX* WITH!
RRRR

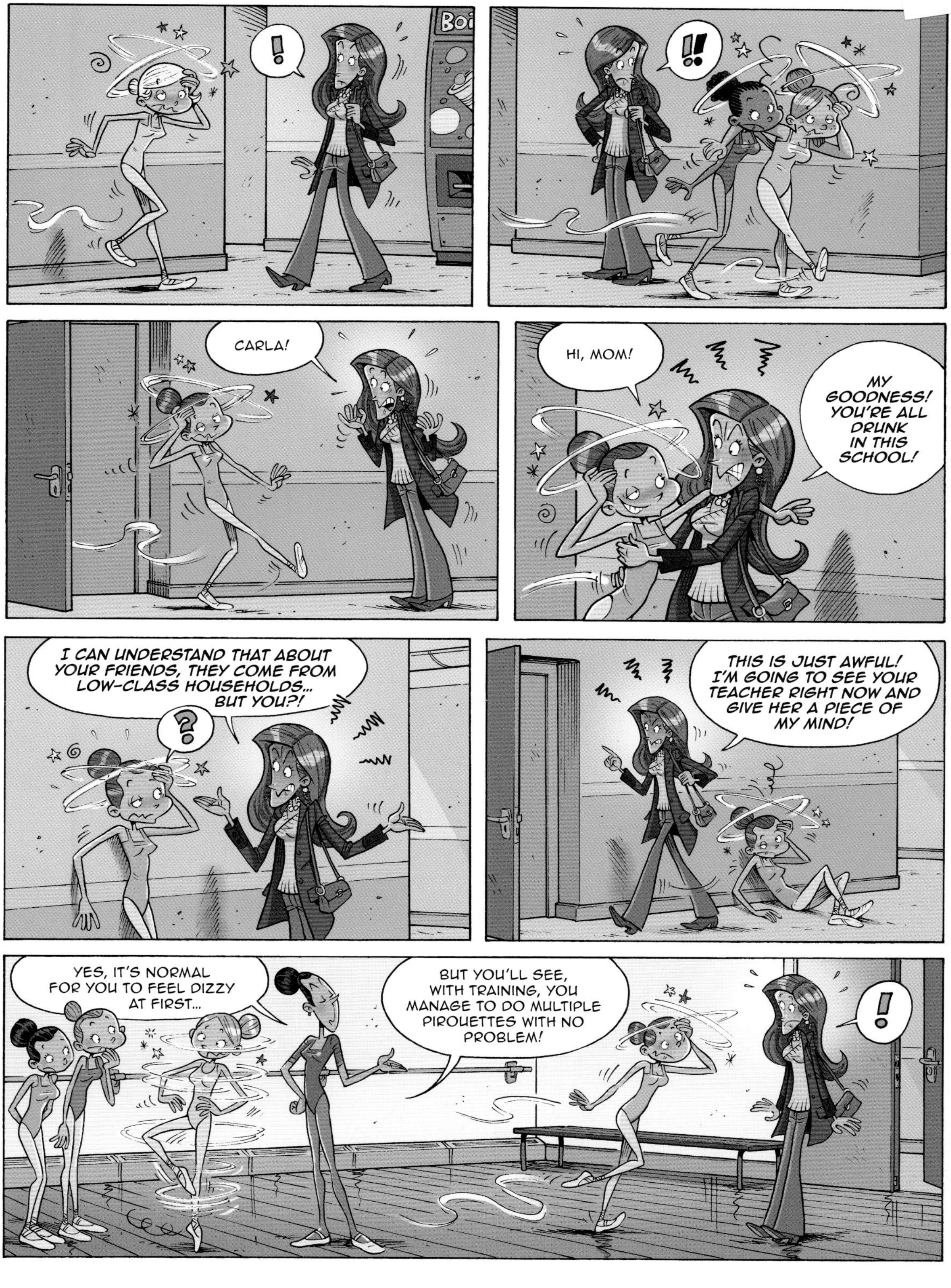
!
!!
CARLA!
HI, MOM!
MY GOODNESS! YOU'RE ALL DRUNK IN THIS SCHOOL!
I CAN UNDERSTAND THAT ABOUT YOUR FRIENDS, THEY COME FROM LOW-CLASS HOUSEHOLDS... BUT YOU?!
?
THIS IS JUST AWFUL! I'M GOING TO SEE YOUR TEACHER RIGHT NOW AND GIVE HER A PIECE OF MY MIND!
YES, IT'S NORMAL FOR YOU TO FEEL DIZZY AT FIRST...
BUT YOU'LL SEE, WITH TRAINING, YOU MANAGE TO DO MULTIPLE PIROUETTES WITH NO PROBLEM!
!

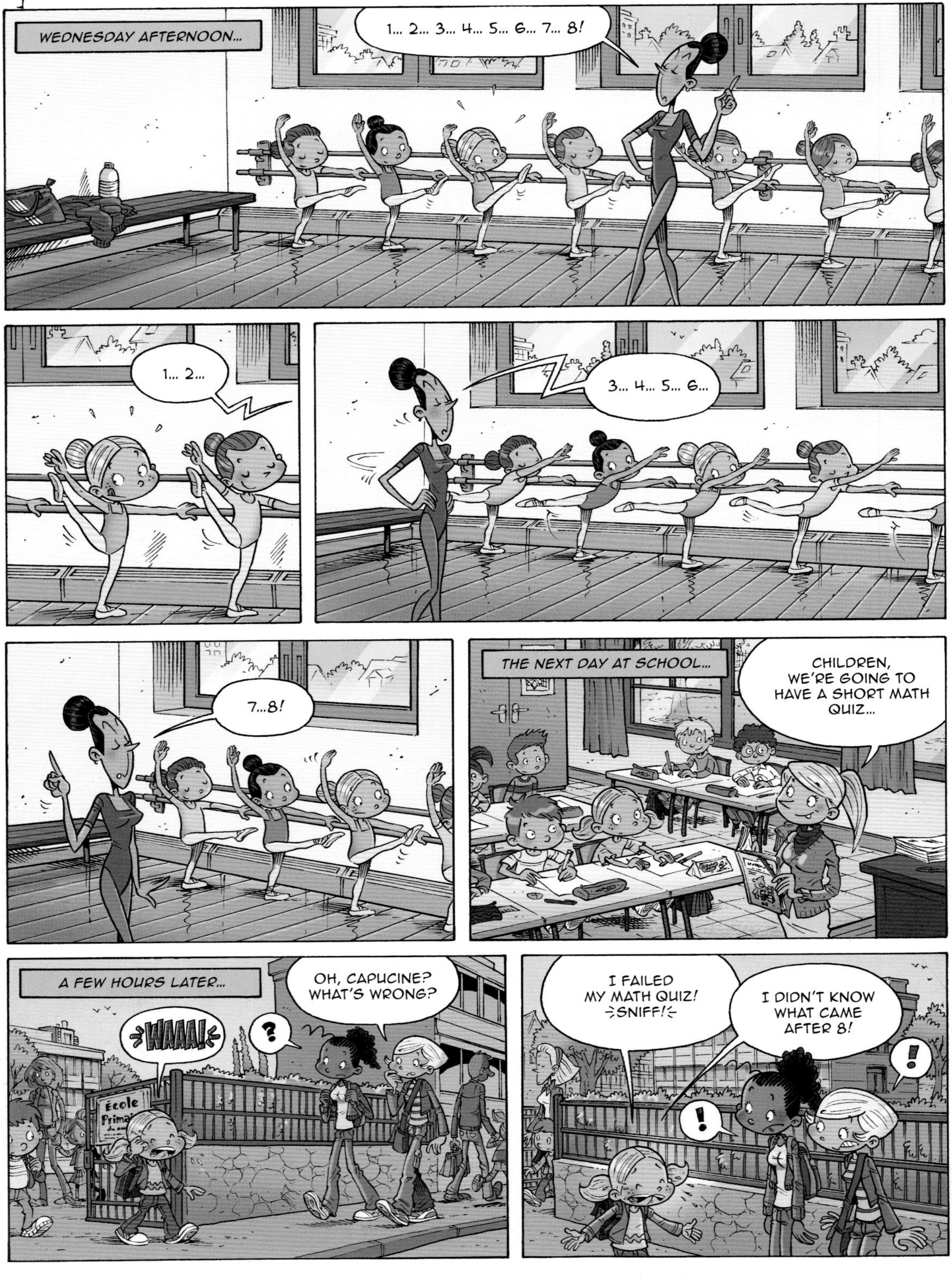
WEDNESDAY AFTERNOON...
1... 2... 3... 4... 5... 6... 7... 8!
1... 2...
3... 4... 5... 6...
7...8!
THE NEXT DAY AT SCHOOL...
CHILDREN, WE'RE GOING TO HAVE A SHORT MATH QUIZ...
A FEW HOURS LATER...
WAAA!
?
OH, CAPUCINE? WHAT'S WRONG?
École Primai
I FAILED MY MATH QUIZ! SNIFF!
I DIDN'T KNOW WHAT CAME AFTER 8!
!
!

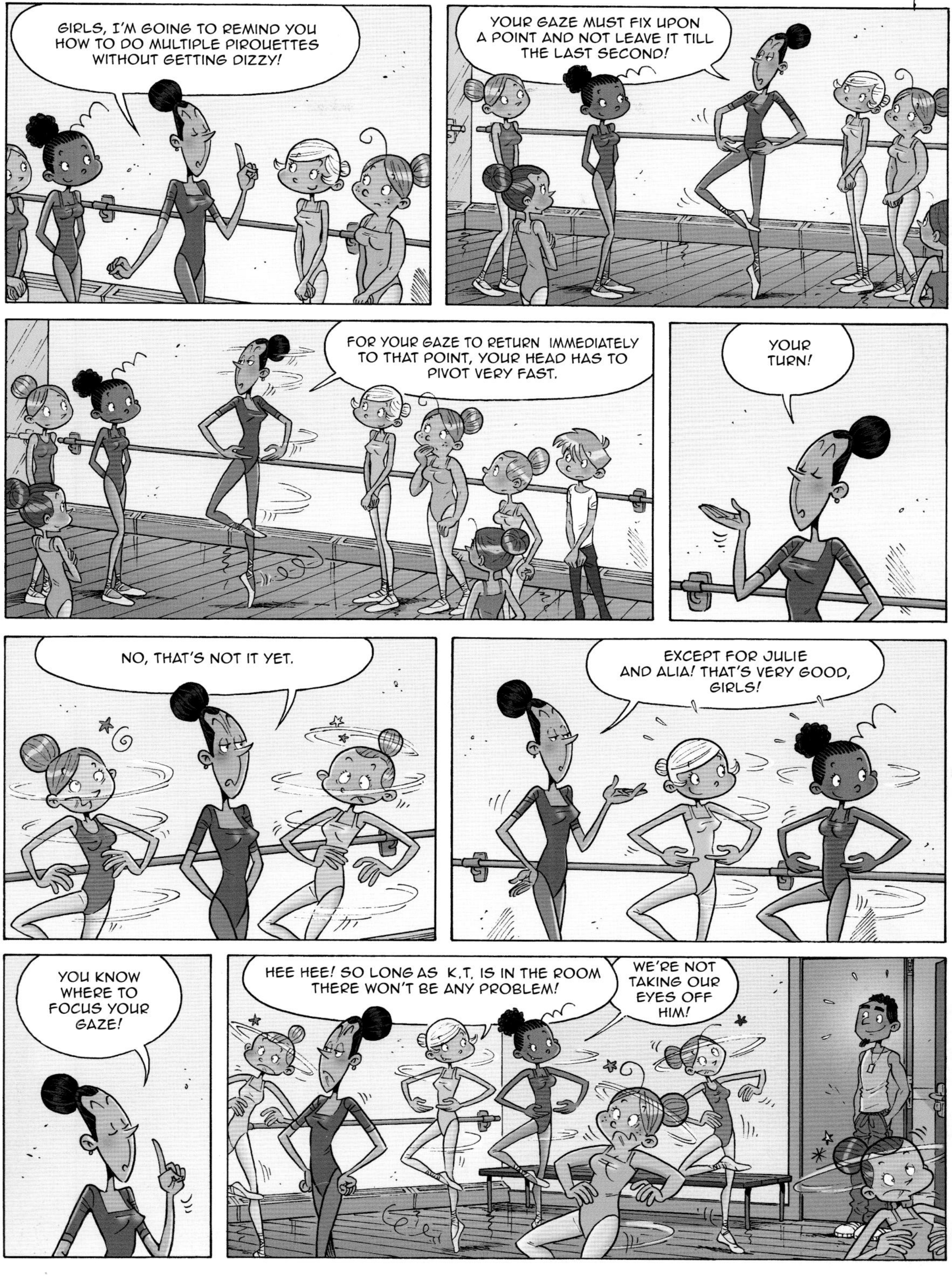
GIRLS, I'M GOING TO REMIND YOU HOW TO DO MULTIPLE PIROUETTES WITHOUT GETTING DIZZY!
YOUR GAZE MUST FIX UPON A POINT AND NOT LEAVE IT TILL THE LAST SECOND!
FOR YOUR GAZE TO RETURN IMMEDIATELY TO THAT POINT, YOUR HEAD HAS TO PIVOT VERY FAST.
YOUR TURN!
NO, THAT'S NOT IT YET.
EXCEPT FOR JULIE AND ALIA! THAT'S VERY GOOD, GIRLS!
YOU KNOW WHERE TO FOCUS YOUR GAZE!
HEE HEE! SO LONG AS K.T. IS IN THE ROOM THERE WON'T BE ANY PROBLEM!
WE'RE NOT TAKING OUR EYES OFF HIM!

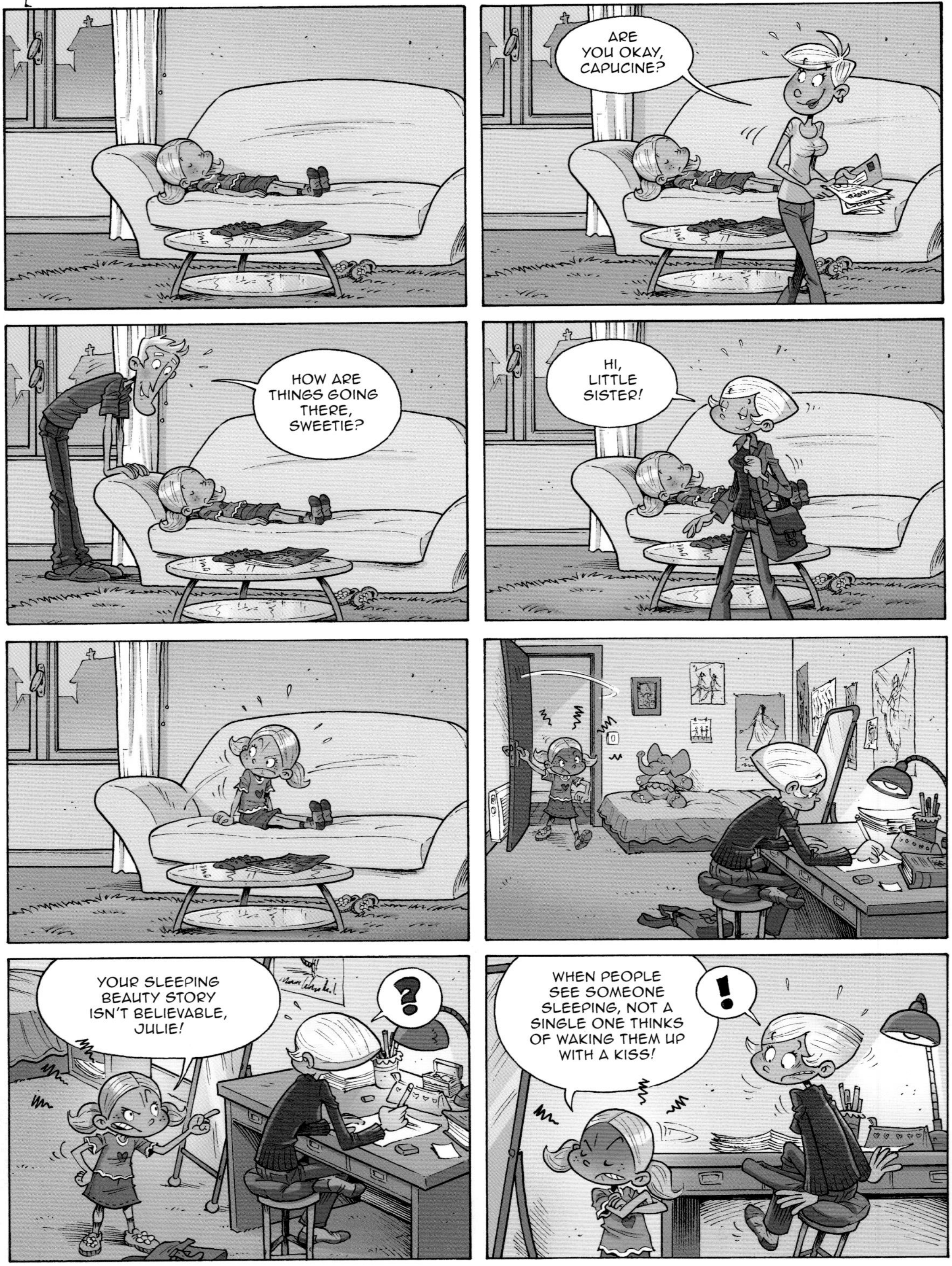
ARE YOU OKAY, CAPUCINE?
HOW ARE THINGS GOING THERE, SWEETIE?
HI, LITTLE SISTER!
YOUR SLEEPING BEAUTY STORY ISN'T BELIEVABLE, JULIE!
?
WHEN PEOPLE SEE SOMEONE SLEEPING, NOT A SINGLE ONE THINKS OF WAKING THEM UP WITH A KISS!
!

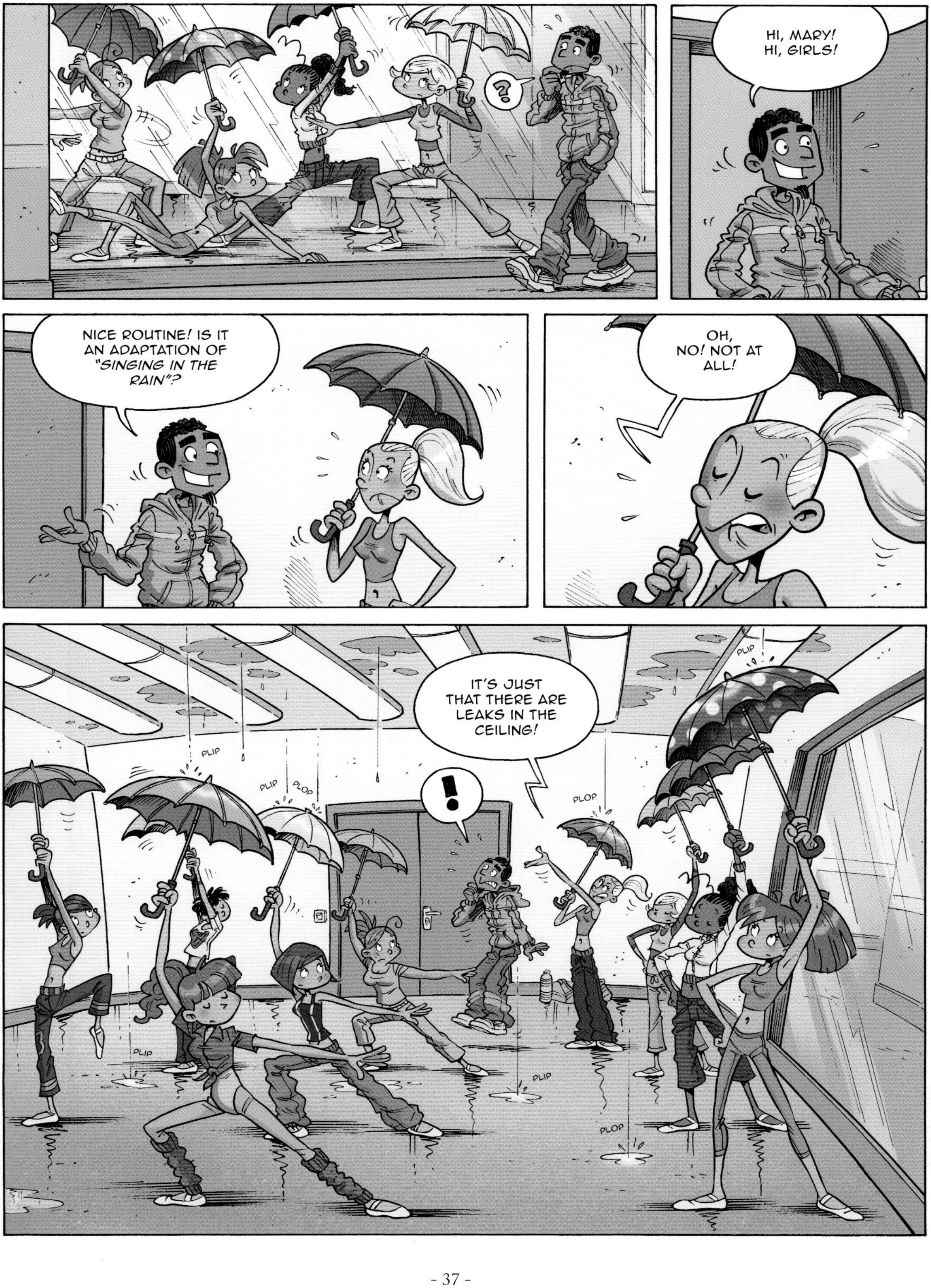
?
HI, MARY! HI, GIRLS!
NICE ROUTINE! IS IT AN ADAPTATION OF "SINGING IN THE RAIN"?
OH, NO! NOT AT ALL!
PLIP
IT'S JUST THAT THERE ARE LEAKS IN THE CEILING!
PLIP
PLIP PLOP
PLOP
!
PLIP
PLIP
PLOP

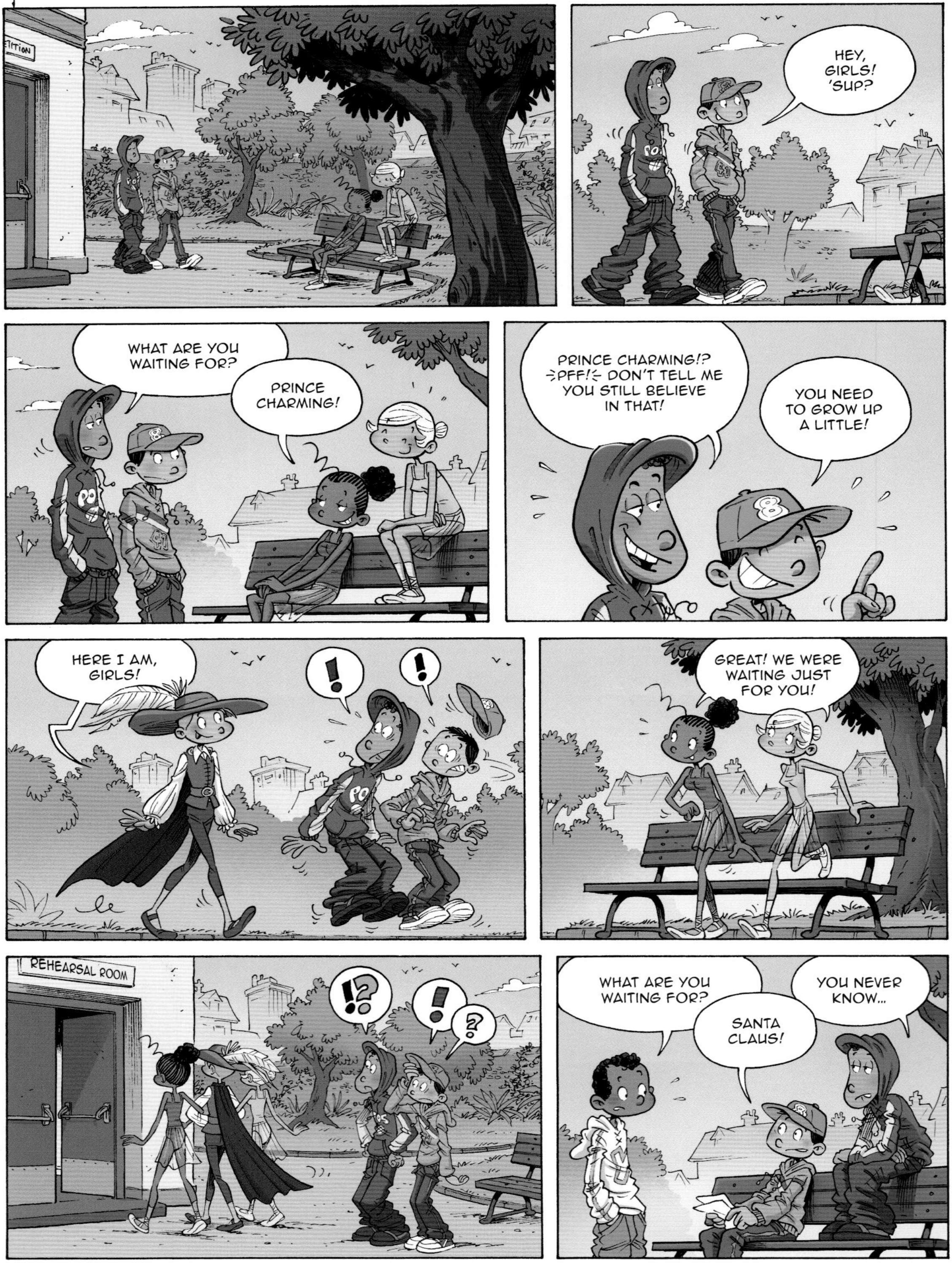

ETITION
HEY, GIRLS! 'SUP?
WHAT ARE YOU WAITING FOR?
PRINCE CHARMING!
PRINCE CHARMING!? PFF! DON'T TELL ME YOU STILL BELIEVE IN THAT!
YOU NEED TO GROW UP A LITTLE!
HERE I AM, GIRLS!
!
!
GREAT! WE WERE WAITING JUST FOR YOU!
REHEARSAL ROOM
!?
!
?
WHAT ARE YOU WAITING FOR?
SANTA CLAUS!
YOU NEVER KNOW...

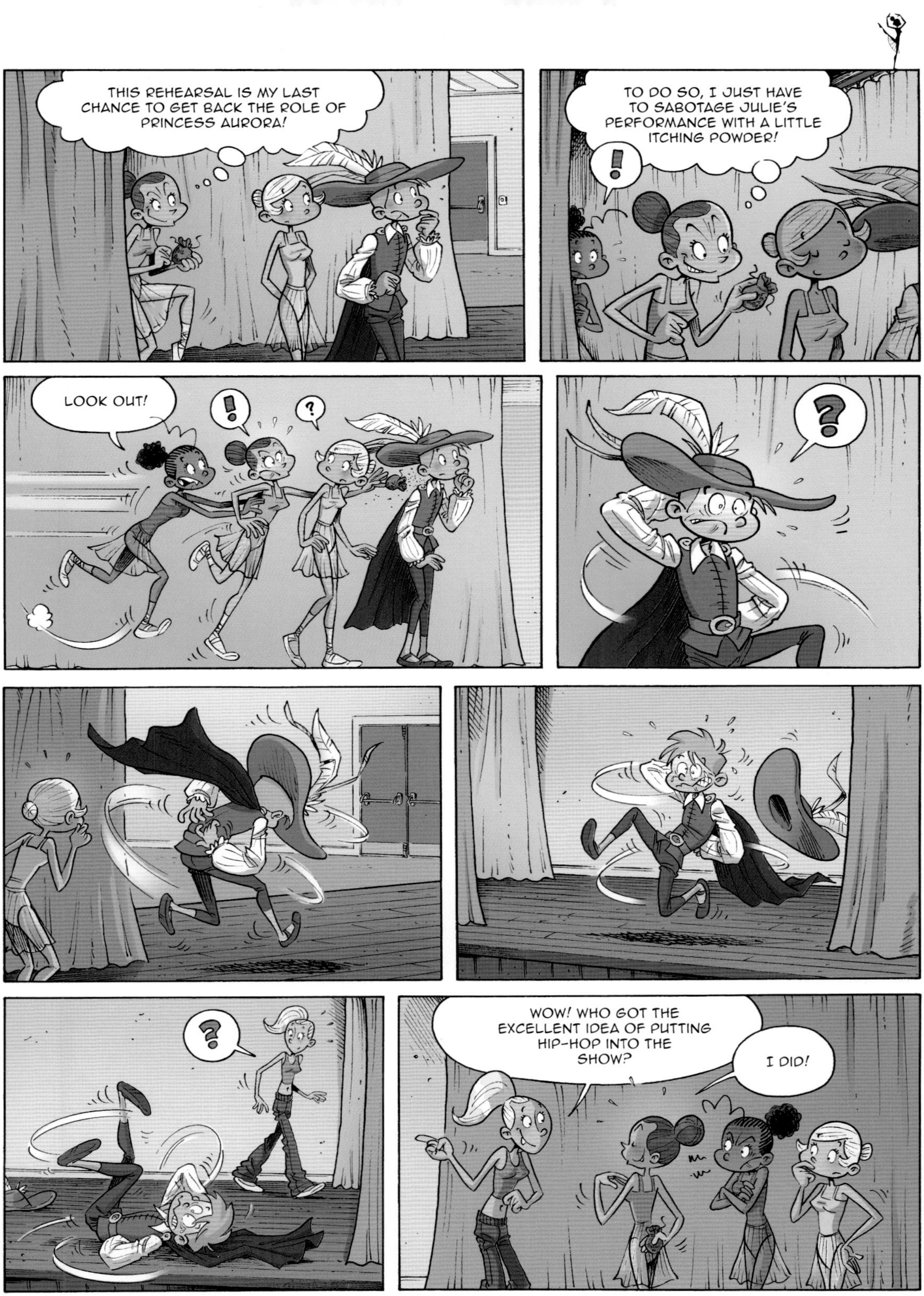
THIS REHEARSAL IS MY LAST CHANCE TO GET BACK THE ROLE OF PRINCESS AURORA!
TO DO SO, I JUST HAVE TO SABOTAGE JULIE'S PERFORMANCE WITH A LITTLE ITCHING POWDER!
!
LOOK OUT!
!
?
?
?
WOW! WHO GOT THE EXCELLENT IDEA OF PUTTING HIP-HOP INTO THE SHOW?
I DID!

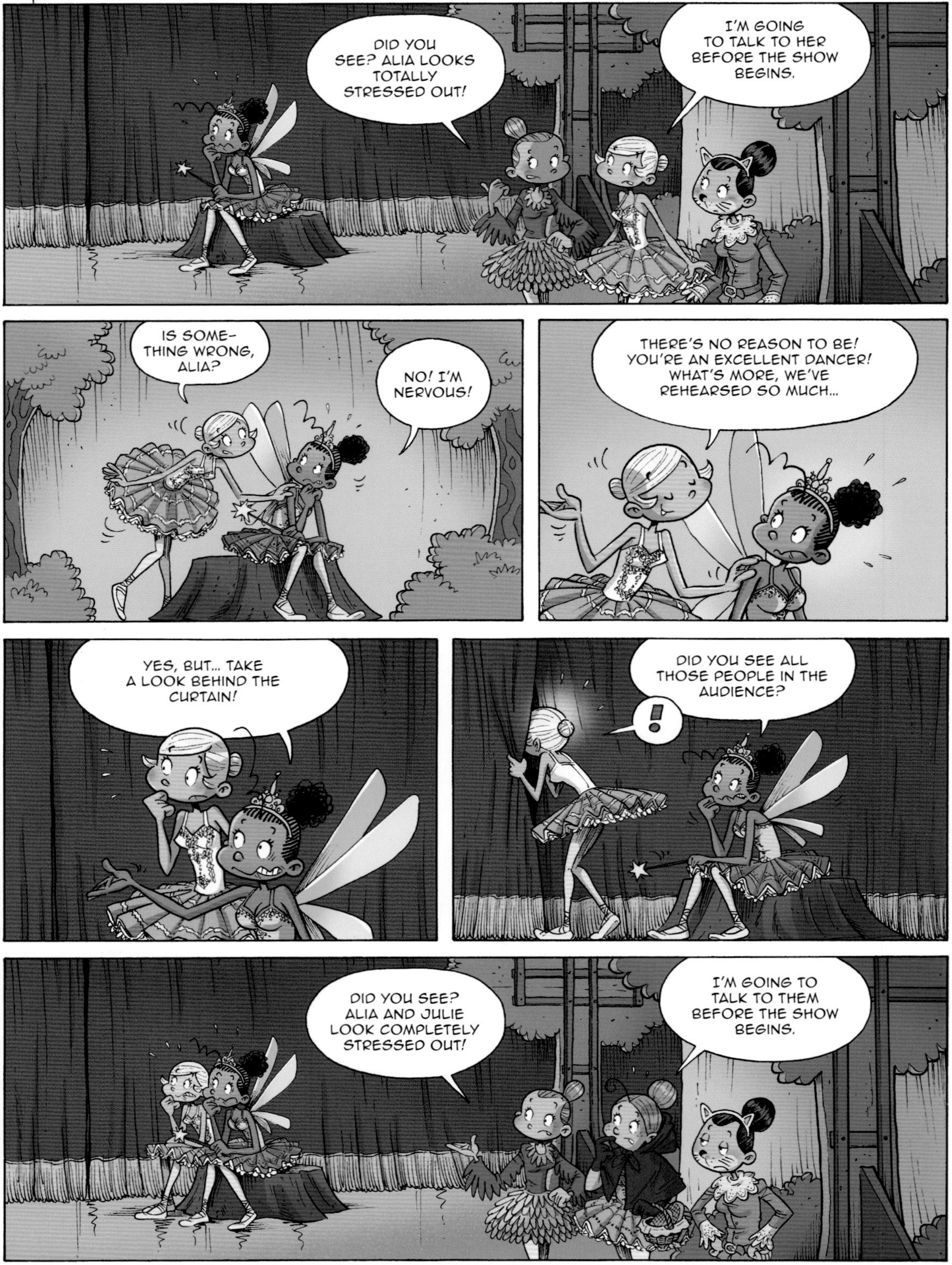
DID YOU SEE? ALIA LOOKS TOTALLY STRESSED OUT!
I'M GOING TO TALK TO HER BEFORE THE SHOW BEGINS.
IS SOME-THING WRONG, ALIA?
NO! I'M NERVOUS!
THERE'S NO REASON TO BE! YOU'RE AN EXCELLENT DANCER! WHAT'S MORE, WE'VE REHEARSED SO MUCH...
YES, BUT... TAKE A LOOK BEHIND THE CURTAIN!
!
DID YOU SEE ALL THOSE PEOPLE IN THE AUDIENCE?
DID YOU SEE? ALIA AND JULIE LOOK COMPLETELY STRESSED OUT!
I'M GOING TO TALK TO THEM BEFORE THE SHOW BEGINS.

Sleeping Beauty

PROLOGUE:

THE BAPTISM OF
PRINCESS AURORA

THAT'S IT! THE FAIRIES ARE DANCING AROUND THE PRINCESS' CRADLE AND SHOWERING GIFTS ON HER!

IT'S YOUR TURN TO GO ON STAGE, CARLA!

YOU MUST SEEM PITILESS IN THE ROLE OF THE WICKED FAIRY GODMOTHER CARABOSSE!

WHILE CASTING YOUR CURSE, THINK OF SOMEONE YOU DON'T LIKE, THAT'LL HELP!

NO PROBLEM!

A FEW MOMENTS LATER...

WHEN YOU'RE 16 YEARS OLD, YOU'LL BE PRICKED AND YOU'LL FALL INTO AN ENDLESS SLUMBER!

BUT THAT'S NOT ALL! YOU'LL NEVER FINISH HIGH SCHOOL!

YOU'LL ONLY DATE LOSERS!

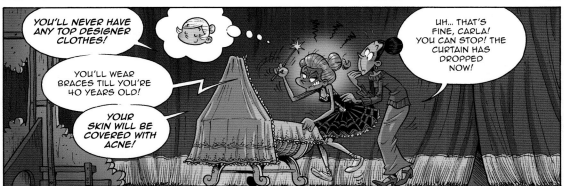

YOU'LL NEVER HAVE ANY TOP DESIGNER CLOTHES!

YOU'LL WEAR BRACES TILL YOU'RE 40 YEARS OLD!

YOUR SKIN WILL BE COVERED WITH ACNE!

UH... THAT'S FINE, CARLA! YOU CAN STOP! THE CURTAIN HAS DROPPED NOW!

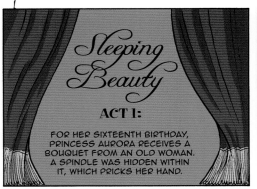

Sleeping Beauty

ACT 1:

FOR HER SIXTEENTH BIRTHDAY, PRINCESS AURORA RECEIVES A BOUQUET FROM AN OLD WOMAN. A SPINDLE WAS HIDDEN WITHIN IT, WHICH PRICKS HER HAND.

BRAVO!

CLAP

MAGNIFICENT!

BRAVO!

BRAVO!

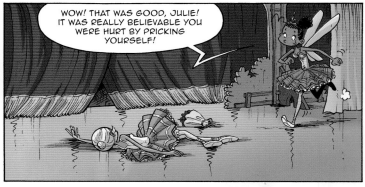

WOW! THAT WAS GOOD, JULIE! IT WAS REALLY BELIEVABLE YOU WERE HURT BY PRICKING YOURSELF!

BUT I **WAS** HURTING!

NATHALIA, THE COSTUME DESIGNER, LEFT A NEEDLE IN MY TUTU!

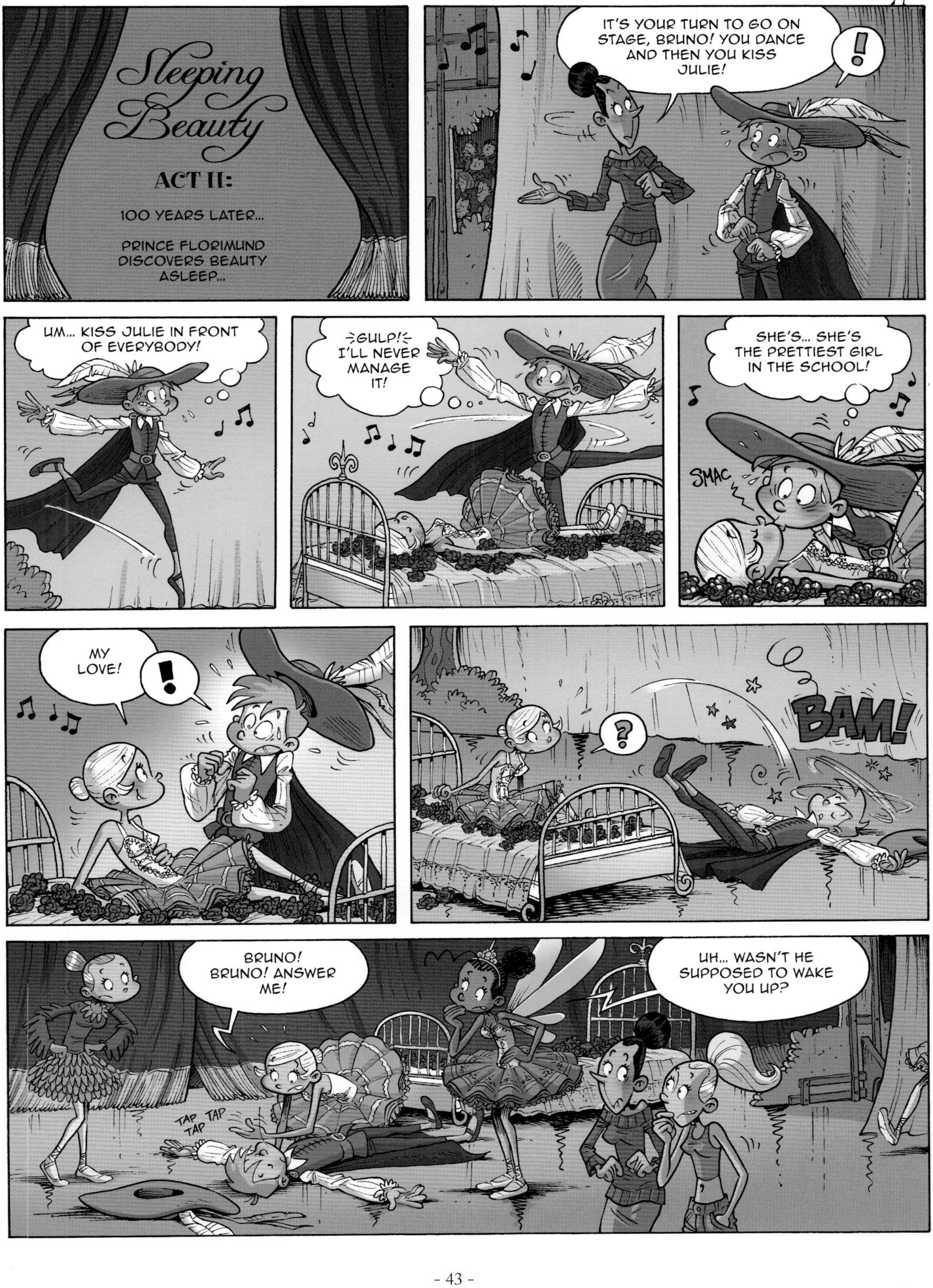
Sleeping Beauty
ACT II:
100 YEARS LATER...
PRINCE FLORIMUND DISCOVERS BEAUTY ASLEEP...
IT'S YOUR TURN TO GO ON STAGE, BRUNO! YOU DANCE AND THEN YOU KISS JULIE!
!
UM... KISS JULIE IN FRONT OF EVERYBODY!
GULP! I'LL NEVER MANAGE IT!
SHE'S... SHE'S THE PRETTIEST GIRL IN THE SCHOOL!
SMAC
MY LOVE!
!
?
BAM!
BRUNO! BRUNO! ANSWER ME!
TAP TAP TAP
UH... WASN'T HE SUPPOSED TO WAKE YOU UP?

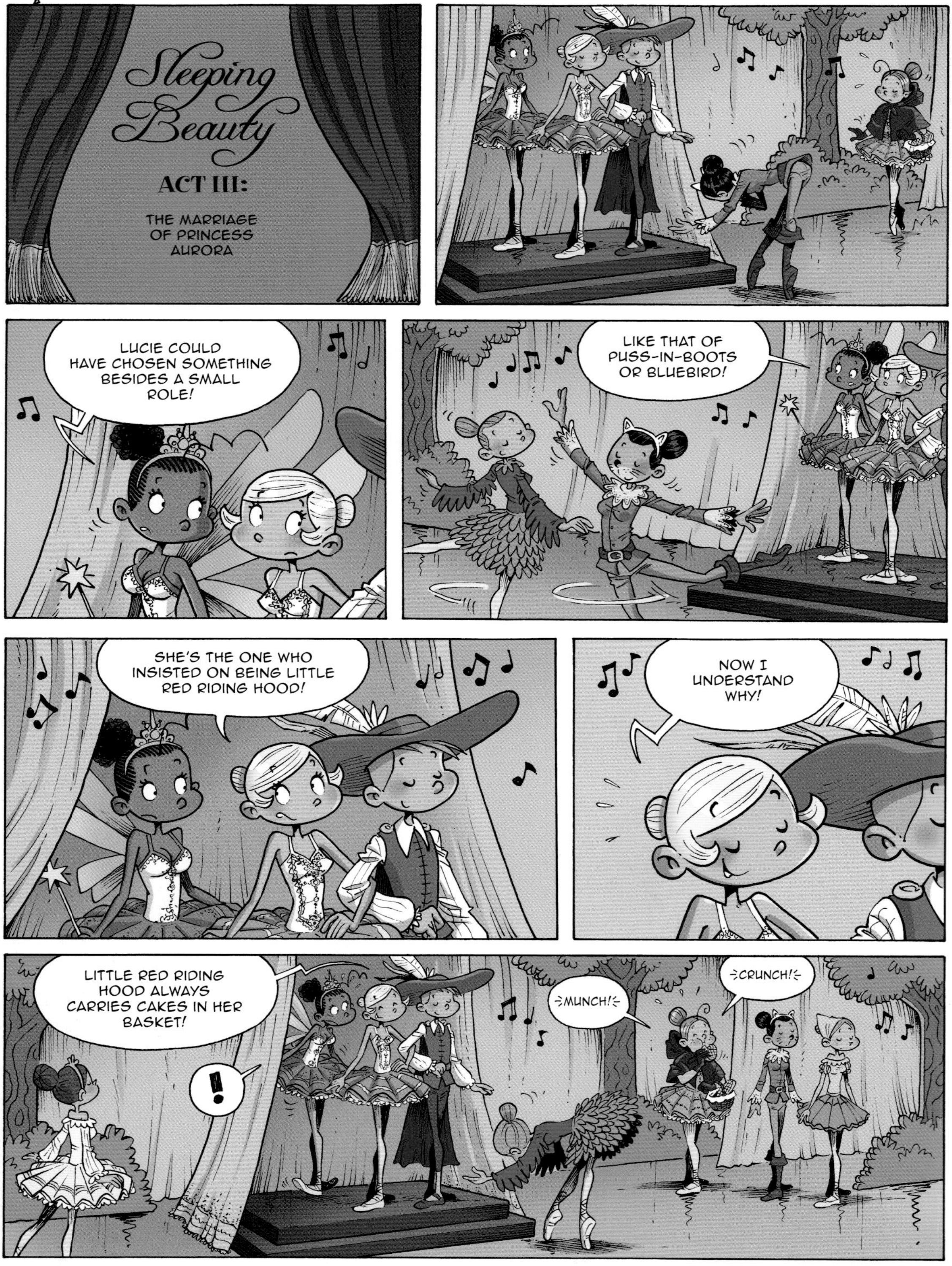
Sleeping Beauty
ACT III:
THE MARRIAGE OF PRINCESS AURORA
LUCIE COULD HAVE CHOSEN SOMETHING BESIDES A SMALL ROLE!
LIKE THAT OF PUSS-IN-BOOTS OR BLUEBIRD!
SHE'S THE ONE WHO INSISTED ON BEING LITTLE RED RIDING HOOD!
NOW I UNDERSTAND WHY!
LITTLE RED RIDING HOOD ALWAYS CARRIES CAKES IN HER BASKET!
!
MUNCH!
CRUNCH!

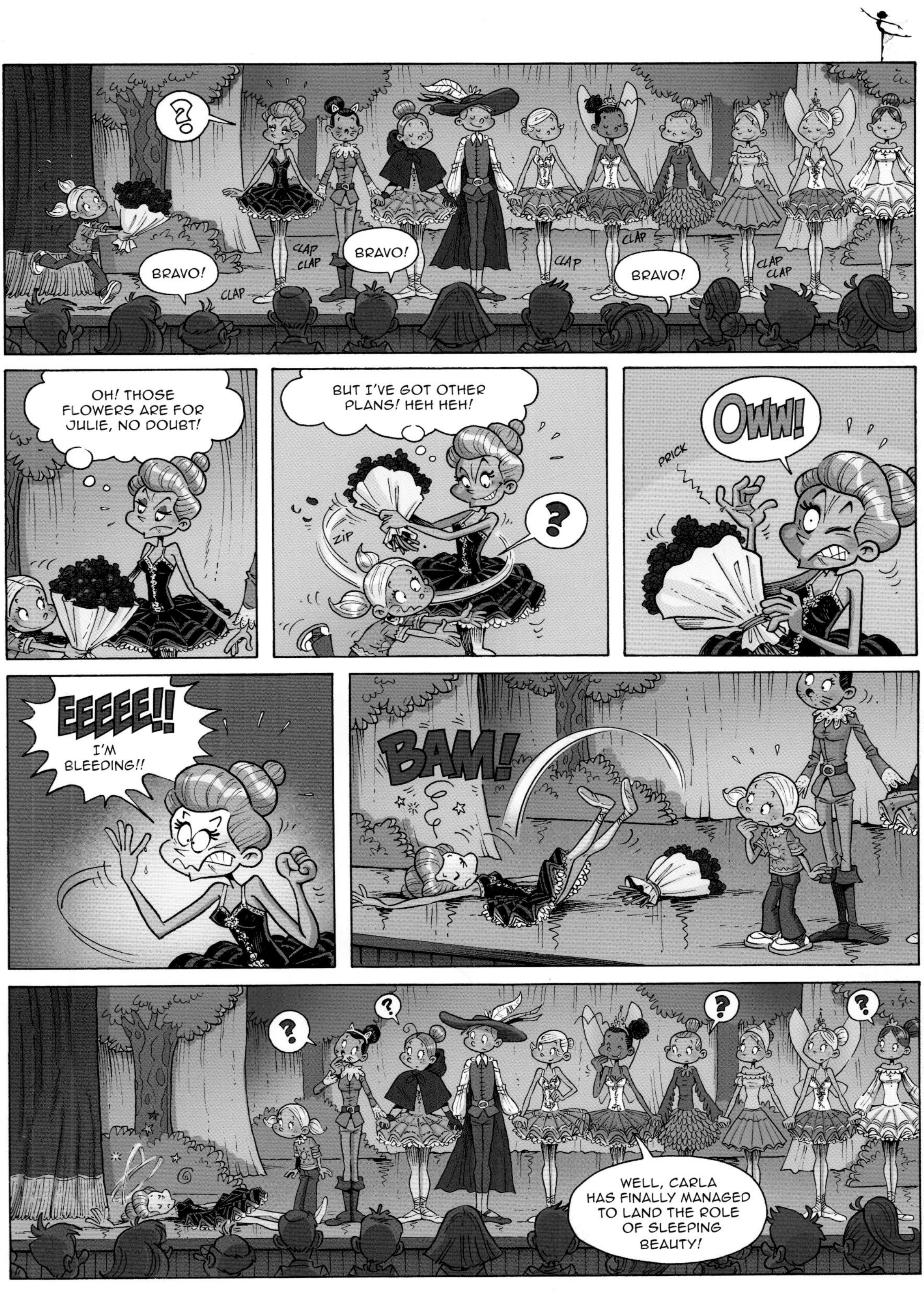
?
BRAVO!
CLAP
CLAP
CLAP
BRAVO!
CLAP
CLAP
BRAVO!
CLAP
CLAP
OH! THOSE FLOWERS ARE FOR JULIE, NO DOUBT!
BUT I'VE GOT OTHER PLANS! HEH HEH!
ZIP
?
OWW!
PRICK
EEEEE!!
I'M BLEEDING!!
BAM!
?
?
?
?
WELL, CARLA HAS FINALLY MANAGED TO LAND THE ROLE OF SLEEPING BEAUTY!

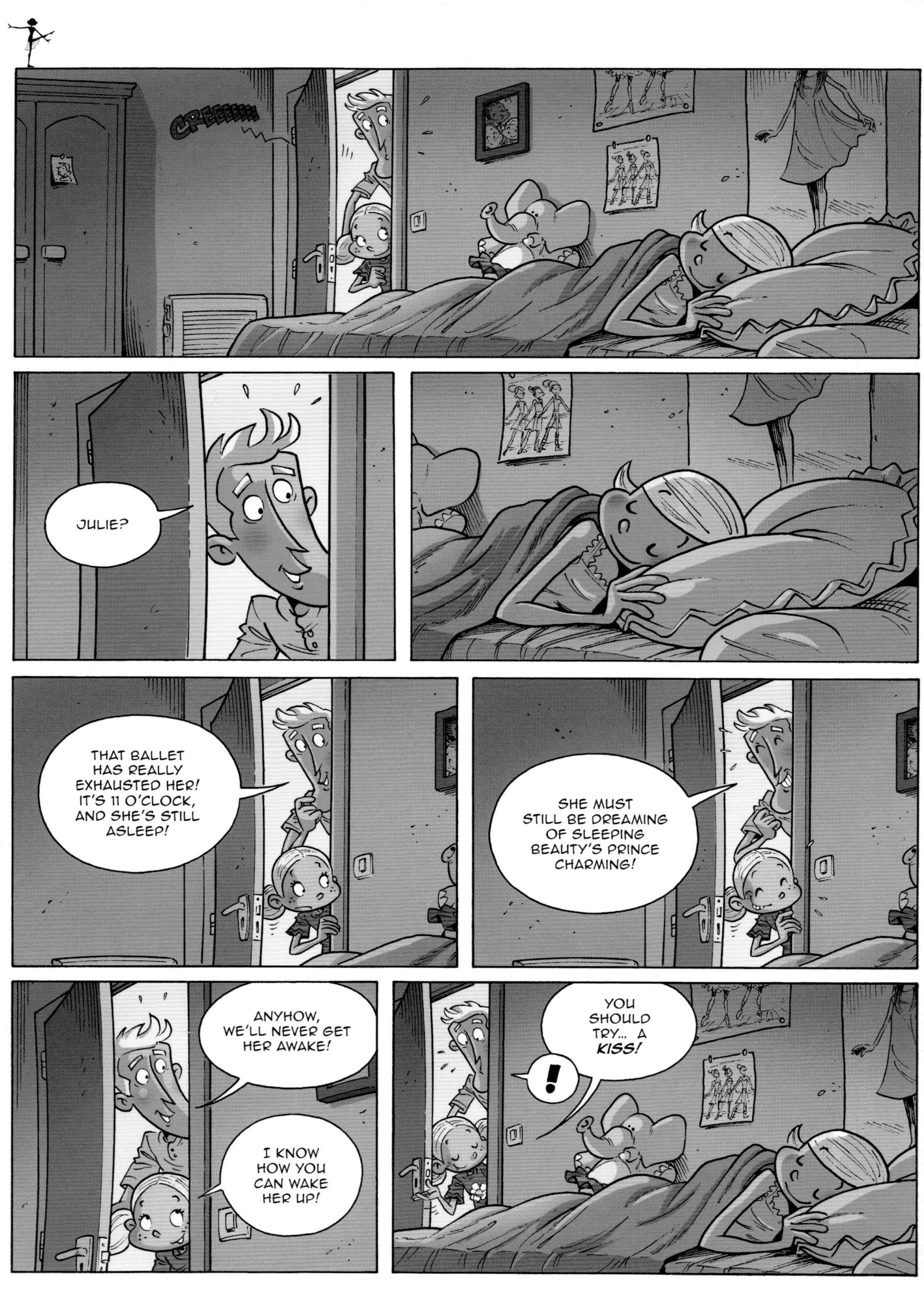
CREEEEEEE
JULIE?
THAT BALLET HAS REALLY EXHAUSTED HER! IT'S 11 O'CLOCK, AND SHE'S STILL ASLEEP!
SHE MUST STILL BE DREAMING OF SLEEPING BEAUTY'S PRINCE CHARMING!
ANYHOW, WE'LL NEVER GET HER AWAKE!
I KNOW HOW YOU CAN WAKE HER UP!
YOU SHOULD TRY... A **KISS!**
!

WATCH OUT FOR
PAPERCUT℣ ™

Welcome to the first DANCE CLASS graphic novel by Crip & Béka from Papercutz. I'm Jim Salicrup, the eternal dance student, who doesn't know an *épaulement* from an *entrechattrois*, and Editor-in-Chief of Papercutz . . . the company dedicated to publishing great graphic novels for all ages. But that has never kept me from enjoying the world of dance or our new DANCE CLASS series of graphic novels!

These days there are all sorts of top-rated TV series featuring exciting dance performances, everything from the celebrity-packed *Dancing with the Stars* to musical comedies such as *Glee*, but back when I was growing up, there were dance shows like what you saw in the movie *Crybaby*—*American Bandstand* and *Soul Train*. I loved those shows! Seeing people move with confidence and joy—I wished I could do the same. But back when I was growing up in the rough and tumble Bronx River Houses, it didn't seem like a very healthy option for a boy. I was no *Billy Elliot!* Ironically, after I moved away, those same housing projects became a vital player in the birth of Hip-Hop. But now anyone can "dance" just by buying a videogame!

While I got caught up in the world of comics, I never forgot about dancing. When the movie *Saturday Night Fever* came along, the disco craze suddenly spread all across America like a pounding, pulsing wildfire. Soon there were disco dance studios opening up every-where, and it wasn't long before I signed up and was stepping on the toes of my poor dance teachers.

Despite my lack of rhythm or any musical talent whatsoever, I stuck with dancing for years, and continue to take ballroom dance classes to this day. Having such wonderful and patient teachers such as Mary Saionz, Tony Musco, and Liz Peterson (who teaches ballroom dance to raise money to help animals—www.dancingforanimals.org) certainly made the process a lot of fun. Even though I'm an average dancer, at best, I still love everything about dancing.

For years I've told friends that dancing is like a form of therapy for me. Because dancing doesn't come very easy to me, each lesson requires a tremendous amount of focus and con-centration—constantly listening to the music, trying to stick to the beat, while leading my dance partner and trying to figure out my next move. By the end of the class it's as if I'd been transported to another world, and when the music stops I return to reality, but refreshed and relaxed, as if I had just taken a short vacation.

Only recently did I finally realize a great obviousity (a word coined by Ms. Saionz)—that one of the reasons I find dance so fulfilling, is that it's the exact opposite of my work! Com-ics are silent and don't move, while dance is all about music and movement! And that makes me appreciate how well Crip & Béka have recreated the feeling of a dance class—capturing the personalities, the spirit, and the love that you only find in the dance world— in this delightful graphic novel series, despite the limitations of the inanimate silent medium of comics.

Chances are you'll enjoy meeting Julie, Lucie, Alia, Bruno, Capucine, as well as Miss Anne, Miss Mary, K.T., and even Carla, as much as I did! And the good news is that the whole gang will be back again in DANCE CLASS #2 "Romeos and Juliet," available soon in better book stores and comicbook stores everywhere! So, until then, keep on dancing (no matter what anyone tells you!)—and don't forget your dance shoes!

Thanks,

Caricature drawn by Steve
Brodner at the MoCCA Art Fest

Check Out These Other Graphic Novels PAPERCUTZ™

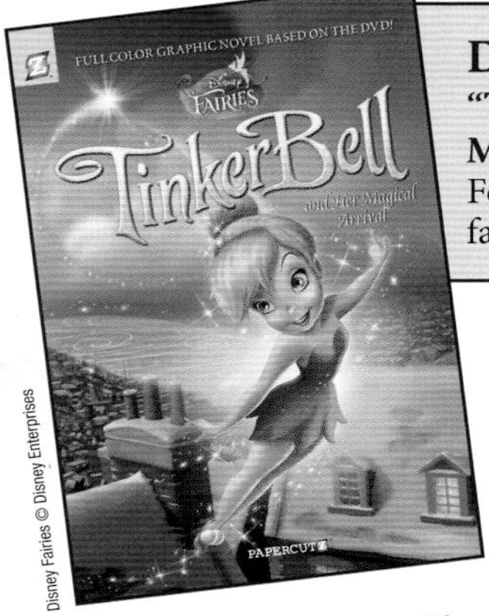
FULL COLOR GRAPHIC NOVEL BASED ON THE DVD!
Disney FAIRIES
TinkerBell
and Her Magical Arrival
PAPERCUTZ

DISNEY FAIRIES #9
"Tinker Bell and Her Magical Arrival"
Four magical tales featuring the fairies from Pixie Hollow!

ERNEST & REBECCA #2
"Sam The Repulsive"
A 6 ½ year old girl and her microbial buddy against the world!

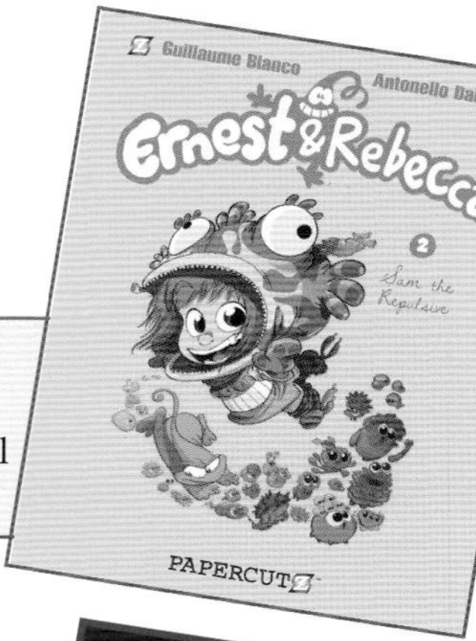
Guillaume Bianco
Antonello Dalena
Ernest & Rebecca
2
Sam the Repulsive
PAPERCUTZ

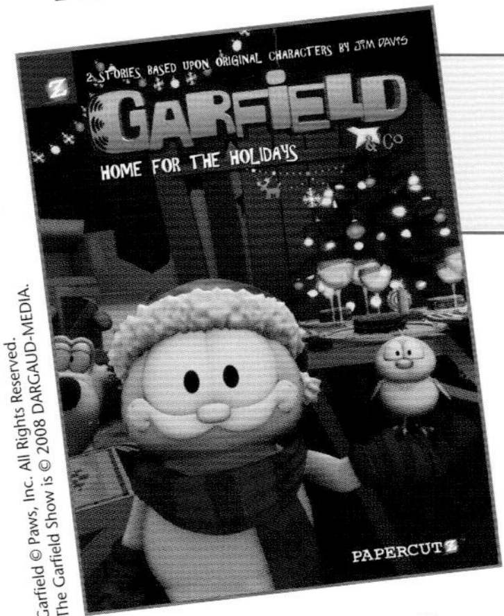
2 STORIES BASED UPON ORIGINAL CHARACTERS BY JIM DAVIS
GARFIELD & Co
HOME FOR THE HOLIDAYS
PAPERCUTZ

GARFIELD & Co #7
"Home for the Holidays"
As seen on the Cartoon Network!

MONSTER #4
"Monster Turkey"
The almost normal adventures of an almost ordinary family… with a pet monster!

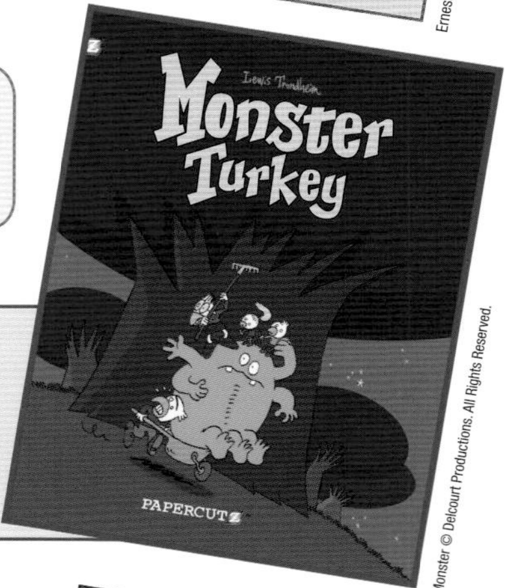
Lewis Trondheim
Monster Turkey
PAPERCUTZ

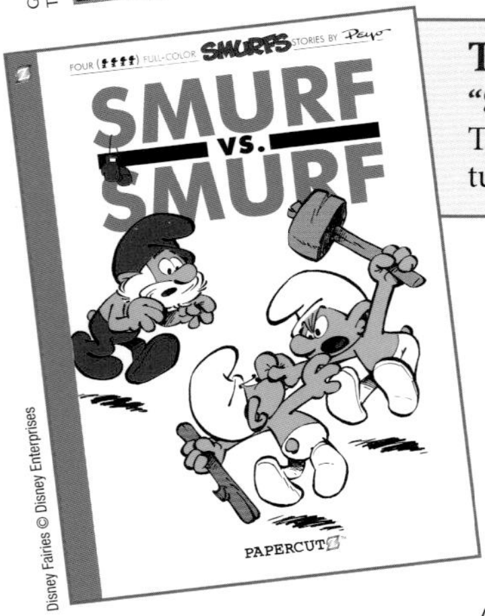
FOUR FULL-COLOR SMURFS STORIES BY Peyo
SMURF VS. SMURF
PAPERCUTZ

THE SMURFS #12
"Smurf Vs. Smurf"
The Smurf village gets turned upside down!

SYBIL THE BACKPACK FAIRY #2
"Amanite"
The adventures of Nina and her fairy friend Sybil!

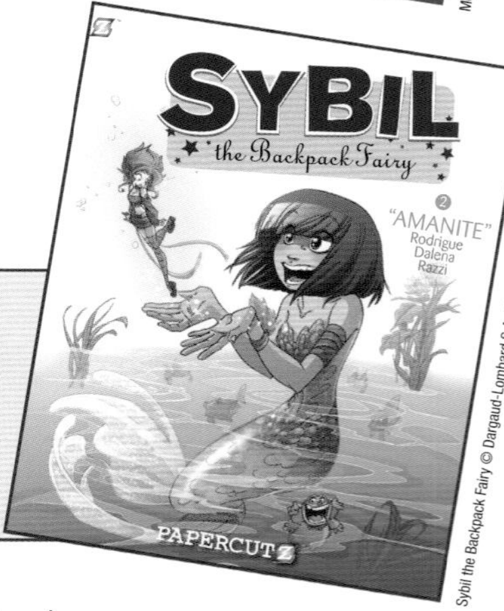
SYBIL
the Backpack Fairy
2
"AMANITE"
Rodrigue
Dalena
Razzi
PAPERCUTZ

Available at better booksellers everywhere!

Or order directly from us! DISNEY FAIRIES is available in paperback for $7.99, in hardcover for $11.99; ERNEST & REBECCA is $11.99 in hardcover only; GARFIELD & Co is available in hardcover only for $7.99; MONSTER is available in hardcover only for $9.99; THE SMURFS are available in paperback for $5.99, in hardcover for $10.99; and SYBIL THE BACKPACK FAIRY is available in hardcover only for $11.99.
Please add $4.00 for postage and handling for the first book, add $1.00 for each additional book.
Please make check payable to NBM Publishing. Send to:
Papercutz, 160 Broadway, Suite 700, East Wing, New York, NY 10038 (1-800-886-1223) • www.papercutz.com

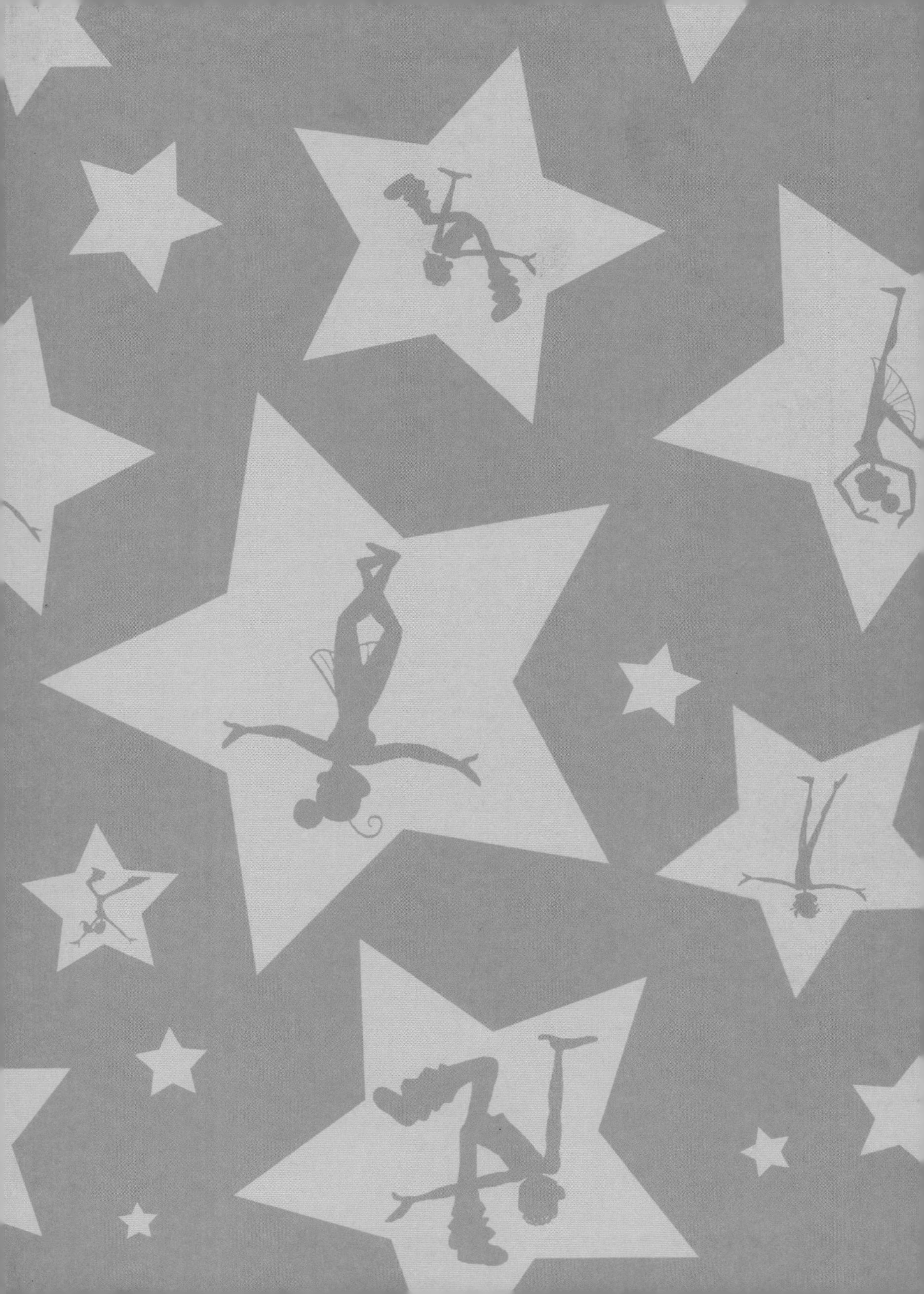